HAUNTED STATES
of
AMERICA

SPIRITS

— ◆ of ◆ —

THE STORM

Book design by Sarah Taplin
Illustrations by Maggie Ivy

Published in the United States by Jolly Fish Press, an imprint of North Star Editions, Inc.

First Edition
First Printing, 2018

This is a work of fiction. Names, characters, places, and incidents are either the product of the author's imagination or are used fictitiously, and any resemblance to actual persons living or dead, business establishments, events, or locales is entirely coincidental.

Library of Congress Cataloging-in-Publication Data (pending)
978-1-63163-212-9 (paperback)
978-1-63163-211-2 (hardcover)

Jolly Fish Press
North Star Editions, Inc.
2297 Waters Drive
Mendota Heights, MN 55120
www.jollyfishpress.com

Printed in the United States of America

HAUNTED STATES
of
AMERICA

SPIRITS

— ➤ of ◄ —

THE STORM

THOMAS KINGSLEY TROUPE

Illustrated by Maggie Ivy

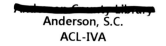

JOLLY
FiSH
PRESS
Mendota Heights, Minnesota

CHAPTER 1

HUNGRY

Sara Leung unwrapped her Meaty Burger with cheese as soon as she sat down. It had been a long time since she'd had one, and she could hardly wait to eat it. Her mom shook her head and gave Sara one of her trademark half-mouth smirks.

"What?" Sara said, holding the juicy burger in front of her lips. "It's been a long time!"

"Yes," Mom said. "But you act like I don't feed you at home, Sara. People sitting near us are going to think I'm a terrible mother, starving her poorly treated thirteen-year-old daughter."

Sara looked around at the rest of the booths in the fast-food restaurant. There wasn't a single person looking at them. Instead, they were biting into their burgers and swabbing ketchup up with their fries.

"No one's watching, Mom," Sara said. "You're just being difficult. Besides, your food is amazing!"

It was true. Her mom cooked traditional Chinese dishes for Sara, her dad, and her older sister, Jess.

Kung Pao Chicken was a household favorite and the golden spring roll recipe handed down from her great-grandmother was legendary.

"Hard to tell sometimes," her mom said with a wink.

"Hey, I love zha jiang mian more than just about anything," Sara said, looking over her dripping sandwich. "But a girl just needs a burger every now and again."

Before her mom could interrupt her again, Sara took a bite. She savored every single delicious morsel. The juicy beef, the gooey melted cheese, the pickles, the tangy sweetness of the mustard and ketchup mixed together. It was heaven on a bun.

"Mmmm," Sara murmured through her mouthful. After she swallowed, she continued, "It's so good it's scary."

"You could write ads for this place," Mom said. She hitched a thumb at one of the promotional posters in the window. It simply read: *Meaty Burger. Where Good Taste Meats.* Beneath the catchy slogan, it showed a picture of an animated burger high-fiving a pack of french fries.

Sara shrugged and took another bite and watched her mom slowly unwrap her grilled chicken sandwich.

It was probably the healthiest thing on the menu. She knew her mom wasn't a big fan of fast food or restaurants in general, but it was a sort of special occasion. As manager of the Galveston, Texas, ValueMart, her mom was in charge of running the biannual store inventory.

Because it was Friday night and Sara didn't have much homework to speak of anyway, she was going to help out. She thought it would be fun to be in the store after hours.

"So, what did you decide about Halloween?" Mom asked, finally taking a bite of her sandwich. "Are you hanging up the mask for good this year?"

Sara smiled. The way her mom said it, it sounded like she used the same costume for trick-or-treating every year. That couldn't be further from the truth. Though she was in seventh grade, she still loved the holiday and wanted to keep celebrating it for as long as she could get away with it. Jess stopped after sixth grade, but that didn't mean Sara had to.

"No way," Sara said. "I can't retire yet. I'll trick or treat until people give me dirty looks when I come up to the door. So, maybe a couple more years?"

"Candy and hamburgers," Mom said. "I'm afraid American culture has influenced you too much."

"Maybe it has," Sara said. "You know, probably since I live here and everything. Besides, it's hard to deny delicious."

Sara finally paid some attention to her french fries and washed a few down with a sip of her orange soda.

She glanced at the dark sky outside the window of the restaurant. Tree branches blew and swayed in the early October wind. Halloween was coming.

"All these scary costumes and decorations," her mom muttered. "I think the store's Halloween section gets bigger and bigger every year."

It was true. Sara was at the store a week or so ago and it seemed as if the Halloween section took up twice as much space as it had the year before. Not only did they have costumes for kids, adults, and even pets, but ValueMart also had an area with animatronic monsters and skeletons.

"I still think we need to get one of those ghosts for our house. We could hang it in the front window," Sara said. "You know, the one with the red eyes and the chains? It makes noise when you walk past it."

"No thank you," Mom said. "Much too noisy for me. And not like the ghosts I was used to as a little girl."

Sara turned her burger around, looking for the next perfect bite.

"Wait, you were 'used to' ghosts?" Sara asked. "What does that even mean?"

"In China we used to celebrate the Hungry Ghost Festival," Mom said. "It was a way for us to worship our ancestors."

"What?" Sara asked. "You guys had a thing where you had to feed ghosts? Last I heard, they don't even have stomachs!"

"You make fun," Mom said, "but it was important to us."

"Sorry, Mom," Sara said, seeing that her words had unintentionally hurt her mother. "How did it work?"

"We would display our ancestral tablets along with pictures of our departed family members," Mom explained. "Then we would put food on the table as an offering to them. We would tell them what we did over the last year. It was thought we'd receive a blessing or a punishment, depending on our behavior."

Sara put her burger down. Mom had gotten her attention.

"Did you ever hear or see any ghosts?"

Mom looked away and laughed.

"It wasn't like the ghosts you see on the TV," Mom said. "It was more like a feeling. Like connecting with the spirits of our past. I could feel the eyes of my ancestors watching us during this time."

"Wow! Do you really believe in that stuff, Mom?" Sara asked.

Her mom picked up her cup of water, thinking it through for a moment.

"I used to," Mom replied after a moment. "It was fun to believe in that kind of thing."

———————

After Sara and her mom finished their meal, they headed to the store. The Galveston, Texas, ValueMart sign was lit up, even if the parking lot was mostly dark. Many of the interior lights were off too. Since the store was usually open twenty-four hours, seven days a week, it was a way of letting customers know that store hours were going to be different for that weekend.

Sara stared at the front of the building as her mom found a parking space up close.

"It looks weird to see the store like that," Sara said. "I'm used to it lit up around the clock."

Her mom turned her head to look up at the sign.

"Yes, but I wish they would've turned off the big store sign," Mom said. "It only confuses people. They're going to think we're open tonight."

They climbed out of the car. Sara made sure to bring her backpack in case she ran out of things to do and decided to work on her social studies paper. She closed

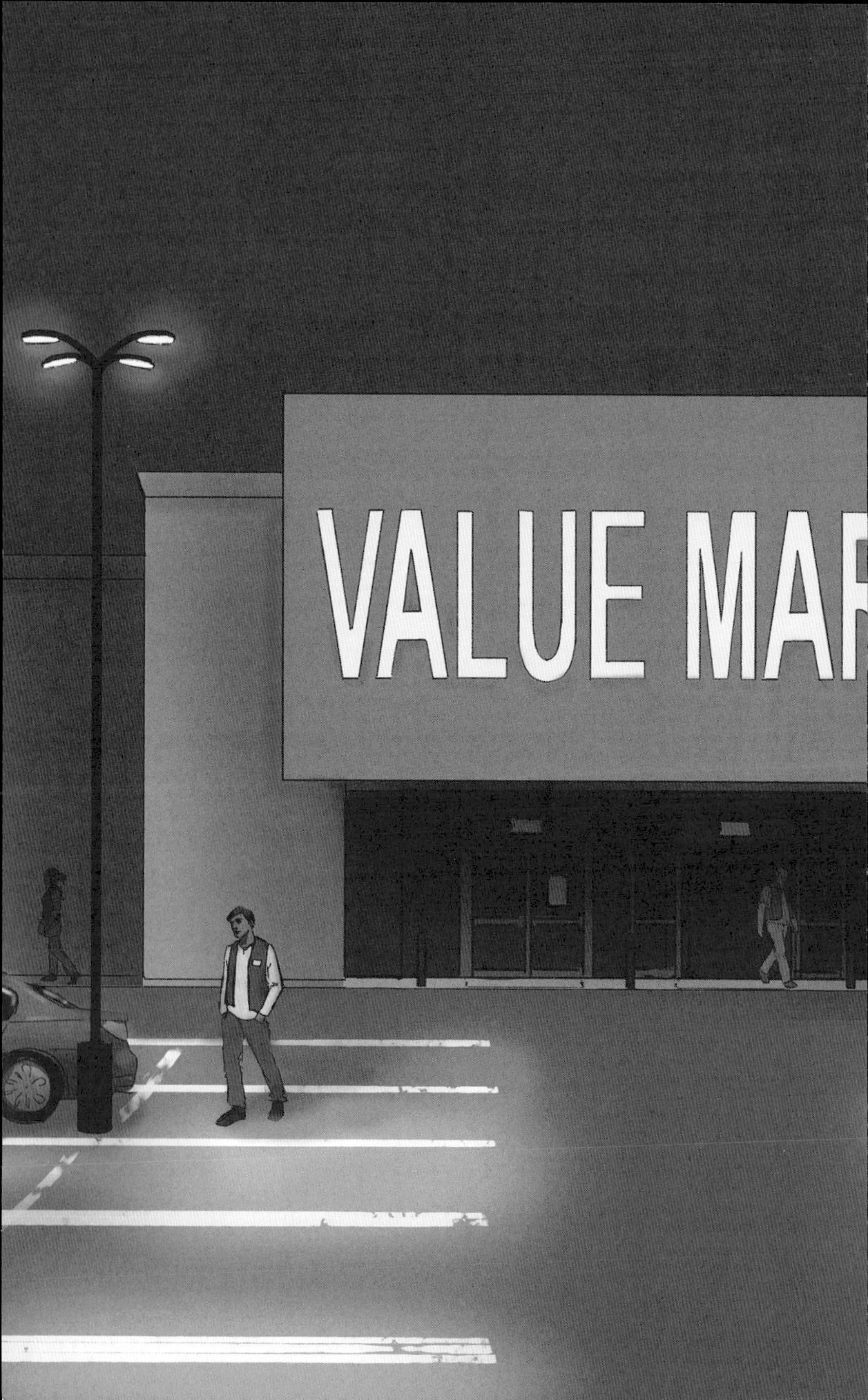
VALUE MAR

the door, heard her mom lock the car with her remote, and they both walked toward the front door of the store.

As they approached, Sara saw a cluster of workers from the day shift coming out. They saw Sara and her mom and smiled.

"Have a good night, Yan," a middle-aged lady with curly long hair called. "Sorry I couldn't stay tonight. My ex is dropping off the kids in a half hour."

"No problem, Rhonda," Sara's mom said with a wave. "I brought some extra help with me."

Sara gave a quick wave, knowing her mom meant that she was the extra help.

A teenaged girl and a guy walking behind Rhonda made some creepy "*oooh*" noises while looking at Sara. They even made their hands look like claws as if they were monsters trying to scare a little kid.

Very funny, Sara thought. *High-schoolers are dumb.* She wondered why her mom had hired a couple of obnoxious teenagers like that.

"Be careful around the kids," the girl whispered as they passed Sara and her mom.

"Yeah, sure," Sara said. "I will."

Considering she had no idea what they were talking about, she wasn't sure how else to respond.

As they crossed the last bit of parking lot and reached the front entryway to the store, the large ValueMart sign went dark. Sara knew anyone driving along Seawall Boulevard would know that the store was closed.

A tall guy with a bushy beard stood by the door and welcomed them in. The name tag clipped to his blue shirt pocket declared that he was BOBBY. It looked like he was in charge of letting any straggling customers know that the store was closed and to let the inventory crew in.

Sara still couldn't get over how different the store looked with half of the lights out. Some sections appeared downright dark. The grocery area was usually bustling with people moving shopping carts through the aisles. The nearby clothing department looked "shopped hard" as her mom sometimes said, with clothes on the ground and racks disheveled.

She wondered how the Halloween section looked.

"So what do we do?" Sara asked.

"We need to wait until the rest of the team is here," Mom said. "But you can set your bag down in my office if you'd like." She passed Sara the keys to her office.

"Okay," Sara said. She walked along the long bank

of empty cashier stations, including the self-checkout lanes. She nearly ran into a woman she recognized but whose name she couldn't remember.

"Hey Sara!" the woman said. "You going to stay up with us tonight?"

"Hi," Sara replied. "I'm going to try. My mom said she needed someone to help straighten up, so I volunteered to help."

The woman was shorter than Sara and had a crazy nest of curly hair on top of her head. She was carrying a box of what looked like barcode scanners in front of her chest, blocking her name tag.

"Well, that's sure kind of you," she gave Sara a warm smile. "And it'll be good to have the help."

Then she leaned in closer to Sara and said, "But honestly, I don't think there's any way we'll get it all done tonight."

"Oooh, don't tell my mom that," Sara said. "She's hoping this will go quick and the store will be back open tomorrow evening."

The woman shrugged. "Maybe with you here we'll knock it out in a couple hours," she said with a wink.

Sara laughed.

"Shoot, I need to get these up front." The woman motioned to the scanners. "I'll see you in a bit."

Sara waved goodbye, still trying to remember the lady's name as she found the door to her mom's office. There was a two-way mirror in it, allowing Mom to keep an eye on the cashiers and the front of the store. She unlocked the door and walked in. Just like home, Mom's office was nice and tidy. There was a large desk with carefully arranged office supplies, two speakers connected to the computer, and a shelf full of neatly arranged books and manuals.

The only personal touch her mom had added to her work space was a small framed picture of the Chinese zodiac symbol for the rat, the year her mom was born. Mom said that people born under the year of the rat were supposed to be instinctive, alert, and great in business.

Sara set her bag down on one of the chairs and took a deep breath. The clock on the wall said it was 10:05 p.m. The night had just begun, and they were supposed to be there until 6:00 a.m.

Is it possible we won't get all the inventory done in eight hours?

As Sara turned to walk back out into the store, there

was a loud knock on the two-way mirror. It startled her and made her nearly jump out of her sneakers. She went to the door, expecting to find one of her mom's employees waiting to come into the office.

Sara opened the door and peered out. No one was there. She quickly realized the front of the store was completely empty. The employees had gathered around her mom near the market entrance and the rows of shopping carts.

"Weird," Sara whispered to herself.

She looked at the mirror once more before closing and locking the door behind her. Pretty sure one of her mom's employees was messing with her, Sara went to join the rest of the ValueMart inventory crew.

CHAPTER 2

TRICK OR THREAT

"I'm not going to lie," Mom said to her staff. "We've got a lot to do tonight."

Sara listened as she stood with the ten other people who showed up for the late-night inventory shift. Her mom had small maps of the store printed out on half sheets of paper. On them were highlighted areas on each of the sections. She shuffled them and had each of the employees pick one from the stack.

"Oh, great," a middle-aged guy with a dark mustache named Howard mumbled. "Automotive."

Sara wondered why that was a bad pick. Maybe it meant he had to count all the tires and auto parts they had near the service garage.

A teenaged girl with purple hair named Cassie made her choice next.

"Sporting goods and toys?" she groaned. "Seriously? That area is trashed."

"Halloween is part of that section too," Mom said.

"We had to use another aisle to fit all the stuff we had shipped here."

"It's going to take forever, Yan," Cassie whined.

"Sara is here to help out by straightening the shelves," Mom said, nodding at her daughter. "You can start scanning the sports stuff and I'll have her start in toys. By the time you're done with the sports inventory, she should be done straightening up."

Purple-haired Cassie nodded. "Yeah, okay."

Sara watched as the rest of the inventory assignments were chosen. The lady with the box of scanners handed the inventory tools out. As she did, her name tag was revealed.

Marcie! Sara said to herself. *That's right!*

Marcie quickly showed everyone how the barcode scanners worked. There was a green button on the top that had to be pressed for a few seconds. When it made a chirp, it meant it was turned on and ready to be used. She also showed them how to enter in the quantity on the little keypad on top.

As she explained how to do it, sporadic chirping tones filled the space as each of the scanners were activated. A guy named George whacked his hand against his scanner.

"Mine isn't working," he said, holding it up.

"And it won't if you keep hitting it," Marcie said with a friendly smile. She reached into her cardboard box and retrieved another one. She traded with George who powered his scanner up and gave it an approving nod.

"Everyone ready to go?" Sara's mom said, trying to sound excited to get started.

There were a few murmurs from the scanner-wielding crowd.

"Then let's get this done!" Mom shouted and threw her fist in the air as if to rally the troops.

Oh, Mom, Sara thought, embarrassed for her.

Sara stood at the top of aisle C14, the first row of toys, and let out the deep breath she was holding. Cassie wasn't kidding. It was trashed and looked like the store usually did the week before Christmas. There were boxes on the floor. A giant pink rubber ball was out of the bin that usually held it. The pegs that held action figures were nearly empty with most of the them scattered on the shelf below.

"Yikes," Sara whispered.

She supposed staying busy would make the time go faster, so she got to work. She arranged the boxed Leaf

Gurl playsets so that they were all neatly lined up. Sara re-hung all the loose figures. She collected all the small plush characters from the cartoon show 7 *Fuzzies* she used to watch when she was much younger. In one fell swoop, she dumped them all into the box and wedged it where it belonged on the collectibles shelf.

As Sara walked over to retrieve the big pink ball to put it back in the ball cage, it rolled across the floor. It came to a stop halfway down the aisle, but Sara stopped in her tracks.

How did that just move on its own?

She approached the ball, convinced that she'd somehow generated some wind by walking toward it. Sara even looked above the shelves to the exposed metal ceiling. There weren't any heating ducts above aisle C14.

It's nothing, Sara told herself and reached for the ball. As she did, a cold draft made goose bumps appear on her arm. It felt like getting hit with ice cold water from a garden hose, but without the wet clothes.

As she touched the ball, she felt a chill race through her fingertips and tickle her elbow to the bone. Sara audibly shivered and as soon as she did, she heard a childlike laugh nearby.

"Hello?" Sara asked.

There was no response.

She thought maybe it was someone on the inventory team working in the health and beauty section of the store a few aisles over. She supposed it was entirely possible that one of them had a strange laugh.

Sara looked over her shoulder and down the newly straightened shelves to the main aisle. No one was there. She turned to glance down the other end of the aisle and to the back wall where the board games were shelved. There, she caught a glimpse of a small boy wearing a dark jacket and short grayish pants. His back was turned to her, but he appeared to have dark hair, cut short. He didn't look like he could be more than five years old. Strangely, the little boy seemed . . . blurry.

A split second later, he disappeared around the corner.

"Hey," Sara called, "I don't think you're supposed to be in here."

She left the ball alone and walked to the end of the aisle, rubbing her arms to try and warm them. As she rounded the corner, she saw that no one was there.

"Hello?" Sara called. "Please come out. If you're lost, we can help you."

Sara stood at the end of the aisle, peering around the endcap. There was no sign of the boy anywhere.

Great, she thought. *Someone left their kid in here!*

She ran down the main aisle, heading toward the front of the store. As she passed other aisles, she glanced down each one, hoping to catch a glimpse of the boy. Instead, she saw Bobby scanning bottles of shampoo and conditioner.

"Everything going okay, Sara?" Bobby asked.

"I'm not sure," she replied, stopping for a moment. "I need to find my mom. I think someone left their son in the store."

"Well, that's not good," he replied, lowering his scanner. "Where's the kid?"

Sara shrugged. "He was over in the toy section," she

began, looking back that way. "But now I don't know where he is."

Bobby whistled and shook his head.

"I'll keep an eye out," he said. His beard moved a little as he talked.

Sara nodded and kept going. After a few minutes, she found her mom in the women's clothing department, scanning pajama pants.

"Mom," Sara said. "You need to come with me. I think there's a young boy still in the store somewhere."

"Are you kidding me?" Mom asked, following her daughter quickly to the other side of the store.

When they reached aisle C14, Sara pointed.

"I was straightening the aisle up and I was going to put the ball . . ." Sara began.

The ball was gone.

"I swear there was a ball here," Sara said. "One of those big rubbery ones. Pink."

"Where is this boy?" Mom asked.

"I don't know," Sara admitted. "He walked around the corner by the board games and that was the last I saw of him."

Sara led her mom down the main aisle to check the remainder of the toy aisles.

"He's gone now," Mom said, shaking her head.

Yan reached and grabbed a small walkie-talkie off her belt. She pushed a button along the side and a tone sounded on the store's overhead PA system.

"Hey everybody," she said. "Keep your eyes out for a small boy who may still be in the store. If you find him, please bring him to the front of the store and we'll contact his parents. Thank you!"

When she disconnected from the PA system, Mom shrugged and looked back at Sara.

"We'll keep our eyes open," Mom said.

"Okay," Sara said. She couldn't help but think her mom didn't believe her.

Does Mom think I'd make something like that up?

"But let's focus and keep working, okay?" Mom said. "I'd love to finish tonight."

"I will, Mom," Sara replied.

As her mom returned to her section of the store, Sara stood at the last aisle of the toy section. The Halloween section started in the next row. Seeing that the coast was clear, Sara decided to take a quick break and look to see what sort of costumes were left.

She wandered down the aisle and, as with the toy department, saw that the merchandise was askew. She spotted a witch's hat left on the wrong shelf. A toddler's bumblebee costume was on the floor, and a hanging plastic life-sized skeleton was off its hook and just resting against a fog machine display.

She picked up the bee costume and headed down the aisle to where the children's Halloween attire was shelved. There were little police officer outfits, more than eight different princess dresses, and a ninja costume complete with dual plastic swords.

And standing next to the shelf, in a plastic yellow firefighter jacket and helmet, was a small child.

The boy! Sara thought. *He's just playing around now!*

"Hey," she whispered. "Little dude."

The boy stood still, staring at Sara. It was hard to make out any details of his face beneath the helmet. His hands were lost in the sleeves of the over-sized jacket.

"Can you come with me?" Sara asked. "The store is closed, but we can call your parents and help you get home."

She hung the bee costume with the others and took a few careful steps forward. Since he ran off the last time, Sara didn't want to spook the little guy.

"I'm Sara. What's your name?" she asked. She wasn't used to talking to kids, but thought letting him know

she was friendly and interested in who he was might be a good start.

The little boy continued to stare silently, and for a moment, Sara wondered if it really was a kid at all.

Is it some sort of mannequin? Set up to display costumes?

The clothes the boy wore moved ever so slightly, making Sara realize the costume wasn't on some lifeless dummy.

Sara got even closer, close enough to smell the plastic of the small red helmet. Even inches away from the boy, she couldn't see his face, nor did he flinch as she approached.

He's probably scared, she thought.

"Hey," Sara said and reached out to touch the little firefighter's shoulder. "It's okay. I'll help you get home."

As her fingers touched the jacket, the entire costume, helmet and all, dropped to the ground. The plastic firefighter hat bounced on the tiled floor, and Sara gasped and withdrew her hand. There was no one inside the costume. Not even a mannequin.

What. The. Heck. There's nobody in there!

Sara's heart felt like it was pumping gallons of adrenaline through her body. She stepped backward until her heel hit the shelf on the opposite side of the aisle. A hand came to rest on her shoulder and she screamed at the top of her lungs.

She spun around quickly, and a plastic bony hand slipped off. The hand and arm swayed from the shoulder socket as if the entire fake skeleton was fanning something stinky. It was just a decorative plastic skeleton, hanging from a peg.

As Sara forced herself to calm down, she caught her breath and eyeballed the firefighter costume again. She slowly approached the crumpled garment.

Sara bent down and picked up the plastic hat. It was ice cold. In fact, the whole area around the costume felt frigid. As she stood there holding the helmet, she felt the cold begin to dissipate as if it had never been cold at all.

What is going on here?

CHAPTER 3

THE WATCHERS

Sara worked her way through the toy section and the Halloween aisle over the next hour. Nothing else spooky happened and she didn't see the little boy again. She was halfway done with the home furnishings and decor department when her mom's voice came over the speaker system.

"We're doing great everybody," she announced, still sounding like an army captain rallying the troops. "Let's take a fifteen-minute break and then get back to it."

After folding a towel someone had wadded into a ball, Sara returned it to the shelf and headed toward the break room. She saw a bunch of the employees walk out, each with a bag of chips or a soft drink from the vending machine.

"Here," Mom said, handing Sara four dollars. "Try and get something healthy."

"That's no fun," Sara replied with a smile. She thought about mentioning the firefighter costume thing to her mom but wasn't sure there was much point to it. There wouldn't be anything to show her anyway. Besides, her mom might think she was crazy.

She waited for her turn at the soda machine and bought herself another orange soda. At the snack machine, she chose a small pack of chocolate-covered pretzels. The couch in the break room was occupied. There were only a few tables and chairs to sit at and the ValueMart employees quickly took them all over.

I've got a better idea, Sara thought.

With her vending machine treats in hand, she walked back across the store to the sporting goods department. She peered down the aisle loaded with tents and outdoor gear and found a few collapsible camping chairs. With her free hand, she picked one up and headed to the electronics section.

Sara set the chair up and found a switch behind the electronics counter and flipped it on. Like magic, the entire bank of twenty televisions came to life.

"Yes!" Sara exclaimed.

She looked around to see if anyone had heard her or seen what she'd done. She was alone and had all sorts of TVs to herself. She was pretty sure it was the best idea she'd had so far. She found the remote controls and changed all the channels so that the TVs aired the same show.

Sara sat down, opened her treats, and watched an episode of a sitcom from the nineties. Parts of the show were funny, but the laugh track got kind of irritating as it was used almost every time someone said something even remotely funny.

As a commercial came on, Sara couldn't help but feel like she was being watched. She glanced over her shoulder to scan the home goods section. There was no one in the next aisle of blenders, toaster ovens, and coffee makers.

You're just being paranoid, Sara thought, turning back around. *You thought you saw some boy and now you're creeped out by everything.*

Knowing the team's break was going to be over soon, she turned her attention back to the bank of TVs. The one in the upper right-hand corner turned off. A moment later, another one in the middle winked out.

"Hey," Sara cried, and turned toward the department's counter to see if someone was messing with her. The counter was empty. And all the remote controls were still next to their respective TV, right where she left them.

She glanced up again and two more televisions turned off.

"Knock it off," Sara called, convinced it was one of the ValueMart employees playing a prank on her. "You're just mad because you didn't think to do this!"

Sara waited for someone to come around the shelf of audio accessories and cables and admit to playing around with her, but no one did. There was nothing but the murmur of the sitcom and a chorus of fake laughter from the remaining TVs.

She turned around, looking for a sign of anyone nearby. As she scanned the televisions, all but the screen in the middle turned dark. Then the last TV went to a static channel, filling the area with white noise. Sara took a nervous step backward and knocked her camping chair over. As she stood there, stunned, she watched the on-screen volume display rise.

The noise became louder and louder by the second. Sara covered her ears, afraid it was going to blow the speakers out.

"Stop!" she shouted.

And just like that, the final TV turned off.

Sara stood there in the silence. Her ears were ringing, but she wasn't sure if it was from the noise or from adrenaline. Out of the corner of her eye, she saw something and turned. To her right, near the shelves of video games, she could see two young girls peering at her, one peeking out from behind the other's shoulder.

Neither of them said anything and just watched Sara from a distance. There was something different about them; they looked almost as if they were images from an old, fuzzy television. Their eyes looked blurry and they didn't smile. Instead, their mouths were like straight red lines. Though it was hard to tell, their clothes looked old, antique even. Plain dresses made up of dark colors. They wore what looked like old brown leather boots with thin laces.

She looked closer and saw a small boy, different from the one she'd seen earlier, crouching near their feet. He was squatting down as if he, too, wanted to get a look at Sara. Like the boy she had seen in the toy aisle, he wore a dark thick coat with large buttons and a wide collar.

Who are these kids?

"Hi," Sara whispered and put her hand up to wave.

One of the girls covered her mouth as if stifling a laugh that Sara couldn't hear. A moment later, airy laughter drifted to her ears as if it came from some other direction.

"Will you talk to me?" Sara asked. "If you're lost, I want to help you get home."

Just then there was a tone and her mom's voice came on the overhead speakers. Sara looked up as if she expected to see her mom up there, watching her talk to the strange kids she'd found.

"Okay everyone," Mom said. "Break time is over. Let's get back to it. We've still got a long way to go."

The sound of the system disconnecting was loud and jarring. Sara averted her gaze to look at the two girls and the boy. Except she didn't see them anywhere. They were gone.

Thanks Mom, Sara thought sarcastically. *You scared them away.*

"Who are you?" Sara whispered.

"I'm Cassie," a voice replied from the other side of the shelf loaded with sound bars and Blu-ray players.

Sara gasped and felt like her breath was sucked out of her lungs. Her heart beat a mile per millisecond as she looked around to see if another strange little kid had appeared. When she turned around, she saw Cassie, the girl with the purple hair, standing in the main aisle between electronics and home accessories.

"Are you okay?" Cassie asked, hooking the inventory scanner into its belt.

"You scared me half to death," Sara admitted. She put her hand to her stomach as if to tell it to settle down. "Was that you messing with the TVs before?"

"I'm not sure what you're talking about," Cassie said, sounding completely confused by the question. She tilted her head as if that would help make sense of it all. "Before the break I scanned everything in sporting goods and was supposed to do toys next. I traded with Marcie, so now I'm going to inventory all of the video games and accessories."

Sara nodded. "Gotcha. Sorry, I was just watching TV and they all started going crazy on me. I was pretty sure someone was trying to creep me out."

Cassie walked a little closer then looked over her shoulder as if to see if anyone else was listening.

"You mean besides the kids?" Cassie whispered.

"What?" Sara exclaimed.

"You've seen them, haven't you?"

Sara nodded slowly. "Yeah. Who are they?"

Cassie took a deep breath, filling her cheeks, and slowly blew out the air.

"You're going to think I'm crazy," Cassie said. "But I think they're ghosts."

Sara felt like her legs were going to buckle. She put her hand on a shelf to keep herself steady.

Ghosts? How is that even possible? Are ghosts even a real thing?

"I've seen them too," Cassie said. "There are a bunch of people who work here that would tell you the same thing."

Sara flashed back to their walk into the store just hours earlier. *Was that what the high school girl meant when she said, "Be careful around the kids"?*

"There are ghosts in the store," Sara whispered to herself, but loud enough for Cassie to hear.

"Yeah," Cassie replied, tucking some of her purple hair behind her ear. "A couple, anyway."

Sara looked around, wondering if the little watchers were spying on them again. There weren't any small ghostly faces peering from around the shelves or anywhere she could see. Maybe the announcement over the speaker system really did scare them away.

"But why?" Sara asked. "Why are they here? What do they want?"

Cassie shrugged. "Who knows? Maybe they just want to scare us."

Sara didn't believe that for a second. They seemed mischievous and playful, but that couldn't be the only reason they were there.

"Here, though?" Sara asked. "Why haunt a ValueMart? Shouldn't they be in an abandoned house or something?"

She walked toward the back aisle by the dark televisions and looked to the left and the right. There were no little ghostly kids to be found.

"They're gone," Cassie said. "They get spooked easily. Anytime anyone who sees them gets too close, they tend to disappear. It's totally weird."

A thought occurred to Sara just then that made her heart feel heavy.

"So, if those kids are ghosts, that means . . ."

"Yeah," Cassie said. "That means they're dead. I don't know the rules, but you can't really become a ghost until you die."

"How awful," Sara whispered.

"It is," Cassie agreed. "And I think they get bored. They seem to really like messing with us. They'll throw stuff off shelves, make noise, and startle people."

"Do they only come out at night?" Sara asked.

"No," Cassie said. "Some of the day shift people have seen them around. They do a pretty good job of hiding themselves. As far as I know, none of the customers have ever noticed the little spookies."

Sara walked to her camping chair and started to fold it up.

"Has anyone told my mom about this?" Sara asked. "I don't think she knows. At least she's never said a thing about it to me."

"I doubt it. People who don't believe in that kind of thing tend to think people who do are a little crazy," Cassie admitted. "And while I don't love my job, I don't want my boss to think I've lost my mind."

"My mom wouldn't fire you for believing in ghosts," Sara said. "Or saying you saw one."

Cassie shrugged. "An old coworker of mine mentioned it to your mom, but she wasn't interested in hearing it. She probably thought he was crazy or something. So, how many kids did you see?"

Sara did a quick count in her head. There was the one in the toy aisle, the one in the firefighter costume, and the three she'd just seen.

"Five, I think," Sara said. "I mean, if those were all ghosts."

"Five?" Cassie's eyes widened, and she shook her head in disbelief.

"Yeah," Sara replied. "Why? Is that bad?"

"I've worked here four years and I've seen like, two," Cassie replied. "You've been here three hours and you've seen five."

"Well, what does that mean?"

"I could be wrong," Cassie said, pulling her scanner from her belt. "But I think those ghost kids like you."

CHAPTER 4
SLEEP TOO

The last thing that Cassie said—that the ghost children might like Sara—scared Sara more than actually seeing the ghosts. She didn't like the idea that spirits from another time had somehow decided to befriend her.

Why me? What do they want?

Since she no longer wanted to be alone, Sara stuck close to Cassie. They worked together straightening and scanning the video games, controllers, systems, and collectibles in the electronics department. When they were done with that, they inventoried all the televisions, speakers, and accessories.

They saw George struggling with his scanner in the kids' apparel section.

"This stupid thing," he grunted.

George looked around and smacked the top of it with his hand. It beeped then whirred, powering down a second later.

"Hey," Cassie said, "you're going to break that thing!"

Sara followed Cassie over to where George was

standing, between two racks of kids' T-shirts with cartoon characters all over the fronts of them. He looked like he was ready to throw the scanner across the store.

"This thing keeps powering down on me," George said. "No matter what I do."

"Maybe it's the battery," Cassie suggested.

She held her hand out as if to offer to look at it. It seemed like George couldn't give it to her fast enough.

As Cassie looked the scanner over, George glanced at Sara. He shook his head and ran a hand through his shaggy hair in frustration.

"No offense kid," George said, "but your mom is delusional if she thinks we're going to be able to finish this tonight."

"None taken," Sara said. "It seems like there's a lot to do."

She felt weird being the boss' kid, especially when she was working alongside ValueMart employees. Sara knew she wouldn't join in and say: "Yeah, you're right. She's the worst!" but also didn't want them to think they couldn't talk freely around her.

"The battery life shows it has three-quarters of charge left," Cassie said, squinting at the small display on top of the scanner. "So that's not it."

The three of them examined George's scanner.

Cassie powered it on and off a few times. She tried scanning a shelf's barcode, but it gave an error beep and then powered down again. She sighed and held hers next to it to see if there was something wrong in the settings.

"Hey," a woman's voice called from the lady's apparel section across the aisle. "You guys having trouble with your scanners?"

Sara looked over and watched as a middle-aged woman headed their way. She had her steel gray hair in a ponytail. Her ValueMart name tag read RUTH.

"These things are garbage, Ruth," George said. "This is the second one that's acted up on me."

"Mine has been fine," Cassie admitted. "But I'm not sure what's wrong with the ones he has been using."

Ruth reached for her walkie-talkie. "I'll call Marcie and see what we're supposed to do. If we have to keep rescanning, we're not getting done tonight. Yan is not going to be happy."

Sara grimaced, feeling a little like an outsider once again.

As the three of them messed with their scanners, Sara roamed around the kids' clothes a bit, making sure she was still within earshot. It was still hard to believe that the store her mom managed had at least five ghosts wandering around.

Are there more?

Sara straightened things as she went. She found a pair of jeans on the floor and clipped them back onto a small hanger. A baseball cap was with the winter hats and she put it back where it belonged. As she walked around a circular rack of boys' hooded sweatshirts, she saw something move toward the fitting rooms. Sara turned and caught a glimpse for just a moment before the figure disappeared into the maze of clothes' racks.

It's another little girl, Sara realized. It looked like she was wearing a rain jacket over her olden-days clothing.

Her pulse quickened as she wondered what the ghosts were doing. *Are there more? Why me? What do they want? Are they just trying to creep me out? Was what Cassie said true? Do the ghost kids like me? Why?*

Unsure why she was doing it, Sara found herself following the ghost girl. She walked near the fitting room and looked to her right. A display with pajama sets swayed as if someone had walked nearby brushing up against them. Seeing as that was likely where the girl went, Sara followed. When she got to the pajamas, she felt that familiar cold sensation.

Maybe I'm close.

She glanced around and saw the underwear and sock display. The plastic-wrapped packages were swinging left and right from their pegs. As she walked through the narrow lane of clothing accessories, she felt the cold draft again. It was chillier than before.

As she emerged from the aisle, she turned to the right and gasped.

There, standing near the girls' coats and sweatshirts, were at least twenty kids. They stood there, looking at her with sad eyes. Then the little girl in the raincoat turned to face Sara. The girl pointed at the ghost children behind her and her mouth moved as if she was trying to say something.

Except no words came out.

Sara had trouble breathing regularly as fear spread through every inch of her. The back of her neck tingled, and her fingers felt prickly as if they'd fallen asleep. She stood there, wishing she could hear what the little girl was trying to say.

Everyone except the girl in the raincoat stood quietly. Some nodded, but none of them made a single sound.

Sara looked at the children, huddled together in their dark clothes. Their faces were as before: hazy and out of focus, making it hard to see any real detail. She

could tell the girls from the boys, but things like eye color, freckles, and anything else were lost.

"What do you want?" Sara whispered. She considered how that sounded, then rephrased it. "What do you want from me?"

The ghost children didn't respond. A few of them looked at one another as if unsure of what to do.

"Sara?" Cassie called from a few aisles over. "Are you over here?"

The sounds of Cassie's footsteps approaching seemed to make the crowd of ghost children anxious. They looked worried and scared, as if they were going to run at any moment.

"No," Sara whispered, holding out her hand. "Wait, wait. She's okay. I promise."

Cassie rounded the corner and Sara watched as the spirits dissipated into thin air. Where there was once a crowd, there was nothing more than a chilly, empty space.

"Who are you talking to?" Cassie asked as she came up behind Sara. "Your ghost friends?"

Sara turned around.

"Wow," Cassie said. "You look like you've just seen—"

"—about twenty ghosts," Sara finished for her.

Cassie let the arm holding her inventory scanner go limp. Her arm fell to her side like it no longer had muscle or bone in it. Her mouth hung open; she was clearly stunned by that newest bit of info.

"You're kidding," Cassie whispered. "Seriously?"

Sara nodded. "I wish I was. One of them led me over here and they all just stood there, staring at me. I think the one I followed tried to say something to me, but I couldn't hear her."

She walked over to where the spirits had congregated and instantly felt the chill they left behind. Sara wondered if the ghosts that caused the cold were still right there, watching and waiting to see what she'd do.

"I'm having a hard time with this," Cassie said. "I mean, it was bad enough thinking the spirits of two dead kids were wandering around the store. But then you come along and see five and now twenty more?"

Sara stopped for a moment and thought about it. Cassie was right. If there were twenty-plus ghosts, that meant that there were at least that many children who had passed away. And while she didn't know much about paranormal stuff, Sara knew that spirits tended to attach themselves to places.

But why ValueMart? What is keeping them here?

And more importantly, *How many more are there?*

"I don't get it," Sara said finally. "Why are they here? What happened to them?"

Cassie stood there, staring into space as if lost in thought. "I honestly have no idea," she finally replied.

———————

It didn't happen until close to 4:30 a.m. that Sara started to crash. She stuck close to Cassie as they worked their way through the rest of electronics department. They had made a pact not to talk about the ghost kids anymore.

"It just bums me out too much to even think about," Cassie said.

"I agree," Sara said and followed it with a yawn.

After a little while, her mom circled by and saw how worn out and lethargic Sara looked.

"You look terrible," Mom said. It wasn't a new thing for Sara to have her mom just say what was on her mind. "Like one of those zombie men in the movies."

"Thanks Mom," Sara said. "It is almost five in the morning, so there's that."

Her mom made some sort of weird *tut-tut* noise under her breath and waved Sara away.

"Go, go," Mom said. "Go lie down somewhere and take a nap."

Cassie looked at Sara and raised her eyebrows.

Great, Sara thought. *She's going to think I'm getting special favors because I'm her daughter!*

"No," Sara said. "I'm fine."

"No, I'm fine," Mom said and snapped her fingers, pointing to the front of the store. "It's dangerous to work when you're too sleepy. You take a short nap and you'll feel better, ready to work."

"But Mom," Sara groaned.

"Go," Mom ordered.

And just like that Sara walked back across the store, her head down, yawning almost the entire way. If there were ghost kids watching or following her, she didn't even notice. One glance over her shoulder let her know her mom was following her.

"Break room," Mom said. "Lie down on the couch."

"Okay, okay," Sara said. She knew she should've gone to bed earlier Thursday night. She'd almost forgotten how late (or was it early?) she'd be up on Friday evening/ Saturday morning.

Sara walked into the break room and saw it was completely empty. That was the first bit of good news.

The second was that she could turn off the light and close the door. She flipped the switch off, but left the door opened a crack so that it wasn't completely dark in the room. The vending machines gave a soft glow to the room too, making Sara feel oddly safe enough to sleep.

Feeling heavy and tired all over, she sat down in the middle of the orange-and-yellow couch and tipped herself over onto her left side, keeping her body curled into a ball of exhaustion. She used one of the throw pillows to support her head.

In minutes, Sara Leung was fast asleep.

———————

Her dreams were scattered, strange, and suddenly interrupted when what felt like a small, cold hand was placed on top of hers.

"Whoa!" Sara gasped, waking herself. She sat up and looked around the dark, empty break room. According to a quick look at the digital display on the microwave, it was 5:17 a.m.

Her heart was doing cardio boxing in her chest as she looked around the room. Other than the blood rushing to her ears, the only thing Sara could hear was the cooling system cycling in the soda machine.

"Hello?" Sara called. She felt like she'd said that way too many times that night and never got an answer back.

She was alone in the break room.

Sara touched the top of her left hand. It still felt cool, as if she'd pressed it against the inside of a freezer. The rest of her skin felt warm.

After a moment, her heartbeat slowed and the fear that rose up inside of her started to ebb. She stood up and rubbed her eyes. As she did, she glanced at the vending machine and saw a girl with short dark brown hair watching her.

The little ghost stood between the wall and the boxy machine, barely fitting in the small space. She had one hand on the edge of the machine and the other somewhere behind her back. Like the others, she just stood and stared directly at Sara without blinking.

"Come out from there," Sara whispered, feeling her heart race again. "I won't hurt you. Please."

Sara took a cautious step forward and the little girl slid a few inches back into the crack between the wall and machine. A moment later, she was gone.

"I don't get it," Sara said aloud, her voice wavering a little. "What are you trying to do?"

Sara walked over to the machine, and as she had come to expect, felt the coldness of the air. As she looked down, she noticed something scrawled in the dust near one of the front legs of the vending machine. Sara sucked in her breath as she squatted down for a closer look.

Written in very faint letters were the words:

WE WANT SLEEP TOO.

CHAPTER 5

CLOSING TIME

Sara stood and walked to turn on the light in the break room, then took a moment to pull herself together. The ghost kids were no longer content watching her from afar. They were trying to tell her something, even if she wasn't quite sure what that was.

"Sleep," Sara murmured, glancing over at the words written beneath the vending machine. "They want sleep too?"

Think, Sara, she told herself. *What could that mean?*

"Sleep, sleep," Sara whispered. "They want to take a nap? Get some rest?"

Once she said it out loud, Sara realized what the little ghosts were trying to tell her.

"Rest," she said. "They want to be at rest."

It made a bit more sense to her then. In books and TV shows, characters always used the word "rest" when talking about people who have passed away. Rest in peace, eternal rest, or even the expression "put to rest."

The ghosts at ValueMart want to be at rest, but what's keeping them from doing that?

She decided she needed to tell Cassie right away. Maybe she had some ideas about what that could mean or what they could do to help the ghost children.

Sara opened the break room door and emerged near the cashier lanes. At the far end and over near the grocery section of the store, she saw the inventory crew huddled together. Her mom was standing in the middle of them, on her cell phone, looking a little distressed.

Cassie saw Sara and walked over to her.

"How are we feeling, Sleepyhead?" Cassie whispered with a smirk.

"Oh, whatever," Sara said. "What's going on?"

Cassie nodded over to the box of inventory scanners. All of them were put back.

"Are we done?" Sara asked. She didn't think she'd been asleep for *that* long. Last she checked, they still had a long way to go.

"I wish," Cassie said. "Nope. All the scanners decided to stop working. Even mine."

Sara looked around at the rest of the group. They looked unhappy and exhausted. If they didn't get done, it was likely that they would have to come back the next night to finish up. She could tell by the look on her mom's face that it wasn't a good thing.

"So, what's going to happen?" Sara asked. She wanted to tell Cassie about the message under the vending machine, but figured she'd wait until the time was right.

"I guess we're going to go home," Cassie said. "We can't do a manual inventory. It'd take until next month to get it all done."

Her mom spoke up just then and everybody listened.

"Okay, everybody," Mom said. "I just got off the phone with Paul from the store in La Marque. They said they'd let us use their scanners."

"Perfect," Bobby said. "They're only like twenty minutes away."

"That is true," Mom said. "But there is one problem. They need to charge the scanners and our store is going to be open for business in about an hour and a half."

"So what does that mean, Yan?" a woman with dreadlocks named Shonda asked. She had her arms folded like she wasn't going to like what she heard.

"We'll need to finish this up tonight," Mom said. "Meaning we need to come back later this evening, after the day and early evening shift."

There were a series of collective groans from the crowd.

"But it shouldn't take long," Mom added. "We were able to get a lot done in the time we had."

Sara felt bad for her mom and thought about how much she'd hate to be the boss of a whole bunch of employees. No matter what, people ended up getting upset. Even when something happened that was completely uncontrollable.

Marcie volunteered to pick up the scanners at the La Marque store later in the day and make sure they were ready for the next inventory shift. Then Sara's mom talked about how she'd have to manually adjust the numbers for everything sold during the time they were open to keep the numbers accurate.

"I wonder if your ghost kids were responsible for this," Cassie said. "Maybe they made the scanners malfunction."

"That's ridiculous," Sara said. "How is that even possible?"

Cassie shrugged. "How is it possible there are a bunch of ghost kids haunting the Galveston, Texas, ValueMart?"

Sara nodded. "You're right," she said. "Which reminds me: I need to show you something."

———

Cassie crouched down and stared at the words scrawled in the dust beneath the break room vending machine. She didn't say anything for a few moments.

"And you swear you didn't write this yourself?"

Sara shook her head like she was surprised by the question.

"No," she replied. "Why would I?"

Cassie stood up and dusted the knees of her black pants.

"Maybe someone was jealous that you took a nap in here and wrote it," Cassie said.

"What?" Sara cried. "You think someone would sneak

in here and write that? That's almost creepier than the little ghost girl I saw by the wall there."

"I'm kidding," Cassie said. "But that's crazy. It's like they're trying to tell you something."

Sara threw up her arms in frustration. "But what? That they're not at rest? I get it. They're ghosts—"

"And there's a lot of them," Cassie interrupted. "I think I need to look for a new job. This place has gotten eighty times creepier since you've been around."

"Gee, thanks," Sara said.

"They're literally coming out of the woodwork to communicate with you!" Cassie replied. "I don't know if you stirred something up somehow with your glowing personality, but they definitely like you."

"So what do I do?" Sara asked. "How am I supposed to help a whole bunch of ghosts?"

"That's a great question," Cassie said, then visibly shivered as if a chill just passed through her. "But the real question is: How are you not more scared by all of this?"

"Trust me," Sara replied. "I'm plenty freaked out. But mostly I feel bad for these kids."

Cassie went over to the bulletin board that was covered with updates, a calendar, and work schedules. She flipped over one of the pages tacked to the board, looked at something, and then let it fall back down. She turned to Sara and twisted her mouth into a sort of pucker, like she was trying to think of the right thing to say.

"What if these kids follow you home?" Cassie asked. "I've seen paranormal shows where the spirits end up clinging to the investigators and follow them around everywhere."

"Seriously?" Sara asked. "Why would you say something like that?"

"Well," Cassie said with a slight shrug of her shoulders. "It could happen."

Great, Sara thought. *Now I've got THAT thought in my head.*

"Look, I'm sorry, okay?" Cassie said with regret. "I don't think they'd do that. I'm just having a hard time wrapping my mind around this whole thing."

"Me too," Sara replied.

"And honestly," Cassie said. "I'm not looking forward to coming back later tonight. Who knows what it's going to be like now that you've stirred stuff up around here."

"I didn't mean to *stir* anything up!" Sara exclaimed. "I was just straightening shelves, trying to make it easier for you guys!"

And just like that, the bulletin board dropped from the wall with a crash, its wooden frame cracking on the hard floor. The girls jumped with fright. The board teetered a moment, then fell forward, launching loose papers in its wake.

"Whoa," Cassie whispered. "Did you make that fall just now? Or was it your little buddies?"

"You touched it last," Sara said.

"Uh-huh," Cassie replied. "So, please tell me you're going to be here later. You are, right?"

Cassie gave a nervous smile and put her hands together as if she was willing to beg.

Sara stopped into her mom's office on the way to the front of the store to pick up her bag. She opened the door and was surprised to find her mom at the computer.

"So, we're done for the night, Mom?"

Her mom took a deep breath and then let it out, nodding as the air rushed out of her nose.

"This scanner problem is a big problem, Sara," Mom said. "The store will lose another evening's worth of sales because we weren't able to finish tonight."

Sara walked over to the chair and hoisted up her backpack.

"I'm sorry, Mom," Sara said, suddenly feeling like she was responsible for the scanners not working. But she shouldn't keep her mind from wandering.

Was what Cassie said true? Did the ghosts somehow mess with the scanners? Sara wondered, creating even more questions. *Was it because I was there? Am I the first person the ghosts have connected with? And if so, why?*

"Remember that little boy I thought was lost?" Sara asked.

"From earlier," Mom replied, switching off her computer's monitor. "Yes. No one else mentioned seeing him."

"I don't think he was a real kid," Sara said.

"What do you mean? Did you just make that story up?"

"No, no," Sara began. "I think, and some of your workers here do too, that there are ghosts in the store."

Her mom stood up and picked up her coat.

"Oh, that's funny," Mom said. "You always did have the best imagination. Your father and I—"

"Mom!" Sara said, interrupting her. "I've seen the ghosts. There are more in here than you would even believe."

Her mom was quiet as she put on her coat and picked up her purse.

"I shouldn't have told you about the Hungry Ghost Festival," Mom said. "It has you seeing things and believing that there are spirits walking around."

"But maybe they had something to do with the scanners," Sara said. "Maybe they made them stop working somehow."

"Oh, no," Mom said, waving her hand. "No, no, no. It was a long night and we're all very tired, Sara."

And with that, her mom got up and walked to the door.

"Are you coming?" Mom asked, smiling as if it was the end of the discussion.

"Yeah," Sara said. "Okay."

———————

Everyone gathered around the front of the store. It was close to 6 a.m. The opening shift wasn't due for another half hour, so Sara's mom wanted to make sure everyone was ready to leave. When the entire crew was accounted for, they all left the store together.

When the sliding doors closed behind the last employee, Bobby locked them and headed to his truck. Cassie waved to Sara.

"See you later tonight?" Cassie called.

"Not sure," Sara called back, following her mom to her car. "Maybe."

Cassie jokingly glared at her and pointed at the store as if to show she meant business.

Sara shook her head then waved her off.

The ValueMart employees scattered in the parking lot toward their vehicles as the last bits of darkness stretched across the Gulf of Mexico's horizon. Sara listened to the faint sound of waves crashing, just on the other side of Seawall Boulevard.

As her mom unlocked the car, Sara glanced back at the store. She gasped.

Standing behind the sliding glass door of ValueMart's main entrance were about ten ghost children, watching her leave. There were boys and girls, all of them were wearing the same raincoats that she'd seen some of them wearing earlier.

"What the—" Sara murmured to herself. She couldn't believe her eyes. Then louder, "Mom! MOM, you have to see this!"

She turned to see her mom had already climbed into the car.

"What, Sara?" Mom replied from the front seat. "What is it?"

Sara turned back toward the store and saw that all the children were gone. The entryway looked dark and empty.

"Never mind."

CHAPTER 6

A DARK AND STORMY NIGHT

Once they were home, Sara went straight to the kitchen and poured herself a bowl of cereal. The nap she'd taken in the break room had helped a little, but she still felt like she could sleep the rest of the day. Despite that, she was hungry.

Breakfast first, then sleep, she thought. *That seems really backward!*

"Dad and Jess must still be sleeping," Sara said.

"They have the right idea," Mom replied, then mumbled a quick "good night" before disappearing to likely get some sleep herself.

"I think you mean good morning," Sara mumbled.

As she ate her cereal in silence, Sara thought about what Cassie had said. She worried that maybe one or more of the ghosts had followed her home. She didn't know if it was even possible. Still, despite the exhaustion that washed over her, she tried to keep a close watch for anything weird.

Then, in an act of pure sleep deprivation, she bumped her spoon on the rim of her cereal bowl, causing it to drop onto the counter with a clatter. She jumped back and nearly knocked her stool over.

"Calm down, Sara," she told herself aloud.

She glanced around the dark kitchen and didn't see any small faces looking back at her. It didn't feel cold and drafty either.

Sara finished her cereal, rinsed out her orange juice glass, and put them in the dishwasher. Through the window above the kitchen sink, she could see the first inklings of sunrise. She thought it best if she tried to get to sleep before it got too bright out.

After a quick change of clothes, Sara slipped into bed and closed her eyes. Almost instantly, she was asleep.

———

As the sun rose, a sliver of light poking through the curtains in Sara's bedroom moved slowly across her face. Sometime after 10 a.m., it made a bright line over her left eye, enough to wake her.

Sara sat up, still feeling a little groggy. She yawned

and rubbed her eyes for what felt like a half hour. When she was done, she looked around her room. Her bookshelf, desk, and reading chair were all just the way she left them. There were no ghost kids watching her or trying to get her attention.

"Good," Sara whispered to herself. "Stay at the store."

But why are they there? She wondered for what was probably the tenth time.

The question kept eating away at her, making her curious as to what could have possibly happened to those kids that left them to haunt a discount store in Galveston, Texas.

She reached over to grab her tablet off the nightstand. She unplugged it and saw it was fully charged. In moments, the tablet was unlocked and Sara was pulling up a search window.

In the address field, she typed "Texas ghost kids."

The results that appeared listed several stories about ghost kids in San Antonio. Even though she knew it wasn't what she was looking for, Sara went down the rabbit hole and learned about a different haunting.

A bus full of kids stalled on train tracks on a rainy Texas morning. A train approached and didn't see the bus until it was too late. It smashed into the bus, taking the lives of ten children.

"Oh, no. That's horrible," Sara whispered, but found herself unable to stop reading.

It's thought by many that the ghosts of the children killed by the train haunt the area. Cars that were put in neutral have moved uphill on their own. Some believe it's the ghosts of the children who lost their lives, trying to protect others from a similar fate.

Sara read that some people even went so far as to put baby powder on the bumper of their car. They were stunned to find small handprints in the powder, proof that the small ghosts were pushing their vehicle out of harm's way.

"Wow," she said to herself, watching a few videos of people trying the experiment themselves.

Focus, Sara. Not what you're looking for!

She sat and stared at the screen, scrolling by entries that didn't seem to have anything to do with what was happening in Galveston. Sara thought about the kids in the store and how many there were. She closed her eyes, trying to remember anything she could about them.

All of them seemed like they were around four to seven years old. They looked like they were dressed in clothes from another era.

Their clothes . . . They were wearing what looked like antique clothes!

She typed in "Galveston, Texas, history" and hit ENTER.

There was an article that described how the port was established in the 1800s. Sara scanned the story quickly and then hit BACK to return to her search. At the bottom of the page, she found a field that read: PEOPLE ALSO ASK.

Below that were similar searches that others had used frequently. The top one was "What happened in Galveston, Texas?"

Curious, Sara clicked on the link and an article that talked about the Galveston hurricane of 1900 opened. A Category 4 storm struck the coast on September 8, 1900, and it was devastating. Winds reached up to 145 miles per hour. Buildings were torn from their foundations, more than 3,600 homes were destroyed, and somewhere around 8,000 lives were lost. People in the area called it the Great Storm of 1900.

"Wait a second," Sara said after looking at a bunch of old photographs of ruined buildings and water-damaged land.

She pulled up a map that showed where the hurricane struck Galveston. On the map, she could see that almost the entire city was in the path of the storm. She found another map that showed many of the buildings that existed around that time, before the hurricane hit. Sara zoomed in and found several buildings in the town. Stores, saloons, eateries, and homes knocked to pieces and scattered all over the place.

Sara opened a current map of Galveston and found her mom's ValueMart store along the coast. She flipped over to the old map and lined it up to the location where the store would've been in the 1900s. She zoomed in to get a closer look at what existed there over a hundred years ago.

She gasped and felt her heart sink.

"St. Mary's Orphanage," Sara whispered. "No way."

The old map showed the orphanage was on the exact site where the ValueMart store stood.

Sara clicked back to read the story that accompanied the map. According to this source, the orphaned children were huddled together with the nuns who took care of them as the storm hit. The nuns had tied clothesline rope around each child's waist as well as their own, so they wouldn't be separated when disaster struck.

Reading on, Sara learned that around ninety children and ten nuns, or "sisters," died when the orphanage was destroyed by the high winds and crashing waves.

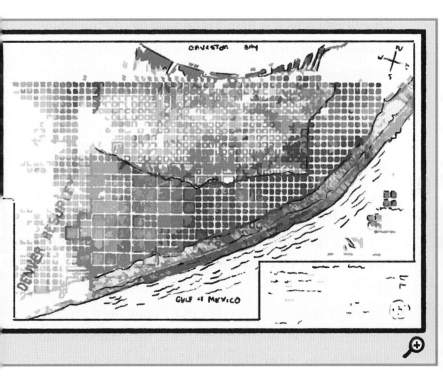

One of the nuns was found across the bay on the mainland, still clutching two children, as if even in death she refused to let go. Only three boys survived the storm.

Sara put the tablet down and gasped, stunned by what she'd read.

All those poor children, just taken away in a single swoop with nowhere to run from the devastating storm, and very little chance to survive.

She felt tears well up in her eyes.

"And now they're stuck," Sara whispered, wiping her watery eyes with her arm. "Trapped on the site ever since."

She wondered what other places had been erected on the site after the orphanage was decimated by the Great Storm. Sara didn't think there was anything "great" about it. If the children were stuck where they'd died back in 1900, did they haunt the other places that had been built where the orphanage had stood?

Sara picked up her tablet again. She did another search for St. Mary's Orphanage. Sites that came up talked about the hurricane and what happened to the children. Unable to read about it without tearing up again, Sara clicked on a link to display pictures. Images appeared that showed buildings before they were destroyed. Though she knew the orphanage was built a long time ago, it didn't look like the building could survive a thunderstorm, let alone a hurricane.

As she scrolled down a little further, she saw old black-and-white pictures of the children who lived in the orphanage. Most of them were wearing bright white shirts. They squinted in the sunlight as their photo was being taken.

To Sara they looked angelic.

She zoomed in on their faces, wondering if she could recognize any of them. The ten nuns who had died trying to save the children were lined up behind them. The nuns had serious looks on their faces. A single priest stood among them, his white collar popping out from his dark robe.

Sara studied every face in the photo. Some of them looked eerily familiar, but she hadn't found any mention of their names in her research. They were a group of doomed, nameless kids who had no idea what fate awaited them.

I need to stop. This is getting to be too depressing for me.

But she found she couldn't.

We want sleep too . . .

Sara wasn't entirely sure what that meant. She still figured that they wanted to finally rest. After being stuck in the same place as that terrible storm for almost one hundred twenty years, she could hardly blame them.

How many people have the ghost children reached out to in all that time? Has anyone even noticed or tried to do anything for them?

She lay back on her bed and looked up at the ceiling. A small tuft of dust clung to its rough surface. It moved a little as air passed by but held fast.

"I need to try and help them somehow," Sara said. "Tonight."

Though she had no idea how she'd even begin to help a bunch of ghost kids stuck in a discount store, Sara knew she had to try.

CHAPTER 7

BACK TO WORK

Later that night, her mom shouted up the stairs.

"Sara," Mom called, "I'm going to go back to the store."

"Okay," Sara called back. "Wait a second."

Sara threw her tablet into her backpack, along with her laptop, a notebook, and a few pens. She put her smartphone into her back pocket. She wasn't sure what else she'd need. Though she'd spent the bulk of her day reading up on ghosts and the kinds of things paranormal investigators used in their investigations, she obviously didn't have any of their fancy gear.

She'd have to use what she had.

Sara came downstairs with her backpack slung over her shoulder.

"Where are you going?" Mom asked.

Sara shrugged as if the question was ridiculous.

"I'm going with you," Sara replied. "I want to help."

Well, I want to help some ghost kids anyway, Sara thought.

"I don't know if it's a good idea," Mom said, her forehead creasing with worry. "You didn't get much sleep after last night and you were acting a little strange with all your ghost talk."

Sara bit her tongue. She wanted to tell her mom about what she'd discovered but knew Mom didn't want to hear it. She wasn't sure if that was her mom's way with dealing with things she didn't understand. Other than Cassie, who wanted her at the store, Sara was on her own.

"I'm fine, Mom," Sara insisted. "You know how I like all of that spooky stuff. I just got a little carried away. But really, I want to help you guys out. The more the merrier, right?"

Mom looked at her for a moment, as if trying to decide whether bringing her along was a good idea or not.

"I don't know," Mom said.

"Oh, c'mon," Sara said. "It's Saturday night. What better way to spend it than at ValueMart helping the store do its biannual inventory?"

Her mom laughed and followed it with a groan.

"If we don't get it done tonight," Mom began, "I think I'm going to quit and sell used cars."

Sara's eyebrows went up. Her mom wasn't the best at telling jokes.

"Err, so that's a yes?"

"Yes, yes," Mom said. "Let's just get in the car already."

As they drove along Seawall Boulevard toward the store, Sara couldn't help but look out her window toward the Gulf of Mexico. Though it was already dark, she imagined what it must have been like in 1900 when people first suspected that the hurricane was going to hit. They didn't have the big, fancy weather detecting devices that are used now that let the world know, sometimes weeks in advance, that a huge storm is coming.

Old-time Galveston didn't have anything even close to that. And even if they did, Sara wasn't sure how they could move nearly one hundred kids out of harm's way.

Her mom turned left onto the street that led to the ValueMart parking lot. Just like the night before, the big sign on the front of the store was illuminated. Sara smiled as her mom shook her head in disappointment.

"Feels like we were just here, doesn't it?" Mom asked.

"It really does," Sara said. She checked out the front of the store as they pulled into the lot. There was a cluster of cars already parked in the lot. She immediately spotted Cassie's small car covered in bumper stickers announcing band names and political views.

Her mom found a place to park, and Sara and her mom climbed out and headed toward the store, ready for another night of inventory scanning and ghost sighting.

Sara was anyway.

ValueMart employees ending their shift nodded at Sara and her mom as they passed. As Sara passed a high school girl (the same one from last night), the girl once again made a face and some spooky sound effects.

"The kids are ready for you," the girl warned. "Look out!"

"Well," Sara replied, "I'm ready for them too."

"Ignore them," Mom said.

"Ignore who?" Sara replied with a smile.

Once inside, they found Bobby at the front door. He nodded at both of them as they entered and bolted the door shut behind them.

"Turn off the front sign please, Bobby," Mom said.

"Oh, shoot," Bobby replied. "Right. Sorry, Yan."

As Bobby made his way to the outdoor light switch to turn it off, Sara followed her mom to the area near the shopping carts. There, Marcie was already passing out scanners.

"I picked these up from the La Marque store," Marcie said. "I did a quick diagnostic on all of them and we should be in business. They're a newer model than the ones we have and operate a little differently, but the concept is the same."

Everyone, including George, seemed accepting of the new scanners.

"You made it," Cassie whispered, sliding over near Sara.

"Yeah," Sara whispered back. "And you won't believe what I found out."

———

"I can't believe it," Cassie said when the two of them had broken away from the rest of the group. "A hurricane took out ninety kids?"

Sara nodded.

Cassie leaned up against a shelf in the hardware section and blew the air out of her cheeks in a long sigh. She glanced up and down the aisle as if expecting to see someone.

"And I bet they're watching us right now," Cassie whispered.

Sara looked down past the shelves loaded with hammers, screwdriver sets, and battery-operated handsaws. She hadn't seen a single ghostly face since arriving at the store. Even though she hadn't been there more than twenty minutes, she began to wonder if maybe the ghost kids had lost faith in her.

Or, based on the paranormal websites she'd read during the day, maybe they'd lost their energy from showing themselves so many times. She'd learned that it took a lot out of spirits to move objects and appear to people in the land of the living.

Maybe they're just all tired out.

"So, this is going to sound crazy," Sara said carefully, "but I'm going to try to help them."

"Really?" Cassie asked. "How do you plan to do that? It's not like you can bring them back to life."

"I know, I know," Sara said.

"And I'm guessing you don't have a ghost-catching device or anything," Cassie said. "Like those guys in the movies have?"

Sara cringed. The last thing she wanted to do was trap the ghost children again. It was bad enough that they were stuck in a ValueMart.

"No, no," Sara said. "I read up on a bunch of stuff about ghosts and I think there's a reason they're stuck here. Maybe they're waiting for someone or something to happen."

Cassie scanned a shelf barcode for a ratchet set. It beeped, and she punched in a number on top of the scanner.

"But don't ghosts always show up where someone died, or where a big accident happened?" Cassie asked. She moved to the next barcode and scanned it too. Sara could tell she was on a mission to get the inventory done tonight, no matter what.

"They do sometimes, I think," Sara said. "But that can't always be the case, can it? I mean, think about it. If a ghost showed up anywhere someone died, there would be ghosts everywhere."

Cassie moved her head back and forth a few times as if thinking it through.

"True," Cassie said. "So why did all of these ghost kids end up here? People are killed by hurricanes every year, I'll bet."

"Well," Sara replied, "I think it's because this was the site of an orphanage back in 1900. All but three of the kids died in the storm."

Cassie gasped. "Really? Wow. That's crazy," she said. "And sad," she added.

Sara nodded, but she wasn't sure anyone knew exactly why ghosts ended up in some places, but not others. Maybe it had to do with big tragedies. Or maybe it was because the ghosts had unfinished business. If the latter was true, then what? What was keeping them there?

"So?" Cassie asked, picking up a clamp to scan it. "Have you seen any of your little friends yet?"

"No," Sara admitted. "Not yet. But I did see a bunch of them standing in the entryway this morning when we left. They were all standing there, watching me, wearing raincoats."

"Raincoats?" Cassie said. "Oh wow. That's so stinking sad. It's like they were waiting for the hurricane or something."

"Yeah," Sara said. "Probably watching and not being able to do anything about it. Then again, it did hit at nighttime. Maybe they couldn't even see it coming."

Cassie sighed, and Sara did too. They both looked at each other and Sara could feel her eyes starting to fill with tears.

"Well," Cassie said in a monotone. "This isn't depressing at all. So glad you came back tonight."

"You told me to!" Sara exclaimed, straightening out the pegs that held hardware for hanging frames on a wall. "But even if you didn't, after reading all that stuff about the Great Storm, I wanted to see if I could communicate with the kids somehow. Maybe figure out what I can do to help them."

Cassie shrugged. "Well, I'd love to see that happen. Even if it does creep me all the way out."

Sara nodded. She guessed she first needed to see if the ghosts would even show themselves to her again. From there, Sara had a few things she thought she could try. One thing paranormal investigators try to do is capture voices on digital recorders or take photos of the spirits.

She tapped the smartphone in her back pocket. It

wasn't the professional gear that the big shots on TV used, but it would do in a pinch. At least she hoped so.

She and Cassie worked together for the next hour and a half with no problems. Neither of them saw anything ghostly as they worked through the hardware section. Sara spotted Shonda and Bobby scanning items in the lawn and garden department.

"Okay," Cassie announced as she slung her scanner into her belt. "I'm going to the little girl's room. You need to go?"

Sara thought that she could probably use a bathroom break, but wanted to test a theory.

"No," she said. "I'm good."

"You going to be okay by yourself?" Cassie asked.

"Of course," Sara replied. "I'm not afraid of ghosts."

"Nice," Cassie said. "Okay, brave one. I'll be back soon."

Sara smiled as Cassie headed toward the front of the store. At that moment, Sara felt the quiet descend on her from the steel struts that made up the store's ceiling. It was almost as if something was waiting for her to be alone.

Just as I thought.

She walked down to the end of the aisle, over to

where a bunch of different toolboxes were on display along one of the walls. She heard a small whirring sound and looked down. A small toy sports car rolled along the floor and came to rest against her foot. Twenty-four hours ago, Sara would've leapt out of her shoes and ran screaming for the exit.

Instead, she looked in the direction the car had come from. A few aisles away, crouched down on the floor, was a little boy in a familiar-looking white shirt and dark pants. He looked up at Sara, his dark eyes staring into hers.

"Hi," Sara whispered, lifting her hand in a wave. "I came back."

To her amazement, the little boy waved back at her.

CHAPTER 8

TINY VOICES

Sara stood in the aisle and felt a cold wave emanate off the little boy. It was like he'd been dipped in a frozen lake and a strong wind was blowing the chill from his little body toward her. In a way, Sara supposed, maybe he had.

The little ghost boy stood up, keeping his eyes fixed on Sara. His arms hung straight at his sides, almost like he was posing for another photo in front of St. Mary's Orphanage. He didn't smile or move. It was as if he was waiting for Sara to go first.

"I know what happened to you," Sara said quietly. "To all of you, I mean."

The boy stood watching her, almost as if frozen in place.

Sara took a cautious step forward and waited for the boy to run or disappear. He didn't do either. He continued to stand there, stock-still.

"I want to help you if I can," Sara said. "If you'll let me."

The little boy nodded.

Sara's heart galloped in her chest. It wasn't fear anymore, but excitement. She was somehow communicating with the boy, even if she still didn't know exactly what she could do for him and the rest of the ghost orphans.

Very carefully, Sara reached behind her and felt the top of her smartphone poking out of her back pocket. Slowly, she removed it. She felt her pulse quicken as she brought it around to her front. She glanced down, touched the home button, and entered her passcode.

Her phone unlocked and the screen displayed all of the apps she'd downloaded.

"What can I do?" Sara asked, looking back up at the boy. "What do you need?"

She tried to keep her eyes on the boy as she pulled up her camera, sure he'd disappear or walk away at any second. For whatever reason, the ghosts last night seemed skittish and ready to dissolve at a moment's notice. Sara just wanted to get a picture of the boy. If anything, to prove to her mom that there really were ghosts in her store and that she wasn't making it all up.

Sara raised the phone and aimed it at the boy, making sure to keep her face in view. She could see his

faded image on the screen. She looked over at him and touched the button to snap the picture.

The boy looked around, as if he was worried that someone else was going to show up. When he seemed satisfied, he looked back at Sara and began moving his mouth. And just as before, Sara couldn't hear a thing he was saying.

She watched him for another moment. The boy stopped talking and then clasped his hands together in front of him.

"I can't hear you," Sara said quietly. "Can you or one of your friends write a message to me again?"

The little boy shifted so that he could look around Sara.

What does he see? Is someone coming?

Sara turned and looked down the aisle where she and Cassie had been working. It was as empty as it was just moments before.

"It's okay," Sara said, turning her attention back to the boy. "There's no one . . ." she trailed off when she saw that the boy was gone, ". . . there."

The sound of snapping gum startled Sara. She turned to see Cassie was back.

"Did I miss anything?" Cassie asked. "Oh, and good

news! Your mom is going to order pizza for everyone in a couple hours."

Sara turned away and felt the warm air return to ValueMart. Cassie had scared the boy away, but Sara felt like she'd made a little bit of progress in the short time she'd had with him.

"I had a little visitor," Sara said, smiling a little. She walked toward Cassie. "And I think I got a . . ."

Sara looked down at her phone. It looked like while she had been trying to keep her eyes on the boy, she'd switched the camera mode from PHOTO to VIDEO. The red button was lit up, an indication that it was still recording.

"You think you got what?" Cassie asked. "I'm suddenly not all that excited for pizza anymore."

"I was trying to take a picture," Sara began. "But I think I got a video of a ghost boy instead."

Cassie's mouth dropped open. She walked over to Sara's side to see what she had captured. As she did, Sara pushed the button, ending the video recording.

A small icon appeared in the lower left-hand corner of the screen, showing that her video had been created and was ready to view.

"Let's see it," Cassie said.

"Okay," Sara said, her hands shaking a little bit. *Why am I so nervous?* Maybe capturing the ghost on video made everything seem real.

Sara tapped the icon to pull the video up. Before she could talk herself out of it, she pressed the "play" arrow.

The video was shaky at first. It then steadied itself and she could see the little boy.

"What the—" Cassie leaned in to marvel at the image of the ghost boy on the phone's screen.

The video started after Sara had asked him a question, so the girls watched as the ghost opened his mouth to speak.

A faint whisper came through the smartphone's speakers.

"He's saying something," Cassie gasped, pulling her hands to her chest. "Oh my god. You can totally hear his voice!"

Sara felt her ears ring as the blood rushed to her head. The back of her neck prickled, and she felt goose bumps pepper the skin on her arms and legs. Cassie was right. There was a tiny voice coming through her phone.

"Go back, go back," Cassie ordered, waving her hands frantically. "Play it again but turn up the volume this time."

Sara paused the video and then used her thumb to wind back to the beginning. She used the button along the side of the phone to raise the volume as high as it would go.

"I'm nervous," Sara admitted, her finger over the play button.

"I'm totally going to throw up," Cassie admitted. "Or pee my pants."

"Please don't," Sara said.

"I won't," Cassie said, pointing at the phone. "Just play it."

Sara pressed play once again. There, just like before, the little boy stood in the aisle, looking at the camera.

"*We want sleep,*" the little boy said faintly. It sounded like a whisper caught on the wind. "*But we can't without our bedtime . . .*"

The last part of his words was jumbled. A moment later he looked over, interrupted by something he saw or heard in the afterlife. Or Cassie coming, snapping her gum. And just like that, he faded into nothing.

"What did he say?" Cassie cried. "Oh, no way. No way. Play it again!"

Sara felt like she'd swallowed a stone. The poor kids

wanted to be at rest. Something was keeping them from it and Sara couldn't hear what it was.

She played the video again and again. Each time, she and Cassie struggled to make out the last few words before the boy disappeared.

"Bedtime?" Sara asked. "Is there a certain time at night they're supposed to go to bed?"

"Heck if I know." Cassie shook her head in disbelief. "This is so freaky. Do you know how crazy this is right now? Can you believe it?"

Sara nodded in agreement. It *was* freaky. She never imagined she'd hear a ghost talking. And to think it was talking to *her*. It was almost too much to comprehend.

Cassie paced up and down the aisle as if trying to figure out what to do with Sara's video footage.

"You could put this on the internet," Cassie said. "You'd get so many hits and get people talking about this. Seriously, this is huge."

Sara ignored the idea of internet stardom. Instead, she tried to imagine the nuns at the St. Mary's Orphanage, getting the children ready for bed. There were close to one hundred kids, and based on the photos she saw, all varying in age.

What was their bedtime? Sara wondered.

"Are you even listening?" Cassie asked. She grasped Sara by the shoulder and looked her in the eye. A strand of purple hair fell across her forehead.

"Yeah," Sara said. "I mean, no. I was thinking about something else."

"You need to post this on the internet," Cassie said. "This will blow up."

Sara thought about it. *What would happen if I put this video online? Would people even believe it? And if they did, would they flood the store, trying to find the ghost kids on their own?*

She didn't like the idea of exploiting a big tragedy just to get some attention online. It didn't seem right.

"No," Sara said. "I can't do it."

"What?" Cassie asked. "Are you serious right now?"

"Yeah, I am," Sara said. "I can't do something like that. A bunch of little kids died a long time ago. The last thing I want to do is make it an attraction."

Cassie looked like someone had punched her in the stomach. "Oh, shoot," she said quietly. "When you put it that way . . ."

Sara shrugged. "I don't mean to make you feel bad, but if you read the articles I found online and saw the pictures of these kids and the nuns who took care of them . . ."

"I get it," Cassie said. "And you're right. You need to keep this to yourself. I don't know what got into me. Maybe too much coffee."

"It's going to be a long night," Sara said. "You'll need all the caffeine you can get."

Sara played the video again and Cassie watched over her shoulder.

"Dang," Cassie muttered. "I wish I would've taken my time coming back. I think it's my fault he didn't finish what he was trying to say."

"You didn't know," Sara said. "But I think they like to talk to me when I'm alone. Almost as soon as you left, he pushed this little car over to me." Sara pointed to the little sports car in the aisle. "It's like he was trying to get my attention."

"Then it sounds like maybe you need to wander around on your own a bit," Cassie said. "Since they like you so much."

"Maybe," Sara said, "but I still don't feel like I'm any closer to figuring out how to help them."

Cassie picked up her scanner and started reading more barcodes. "But at least you know there's a way to listen to what they're saying," she said. "Just keep your phone handy and talk to your little ghost pals. Maybe next time they'll be able to tell you what they want."

Sara shuddered. "I think I'll just keep doing inventory for now." The thought of wandering around the store alone where there could be as many as ninety ghost kids sent a chill through her. She knew they didn't mean her any harm, but it still didn't change the fact that the dead were willing to talk to her.

She just hoped she could figure out what they wanted.

CHAPTER 9

ALWAYS KNEW

The ValueMart crew made great progress over the next couple hours. The scanners behaved themselves and continued to work as they were supposed to, even for George. Sara tried to figure out what the ghost kids wanted from her. She hadn't reached any conclusions.

When Sara's mom called for them to take a pizza break, she estimated that they'd have the entire store completely inventoried within the next hour.

As the crew sat in the break room and ate their pizza, Sara decided she needed to explore the store. Cassie was right. The ghosts seemed to disappear if Cassie or anyone else was around. Though it made her uneasy to wander the store alone, she didn't think there was much choice.

Plus, I'm running out of time.

Sara decided to head toward the lawn and garden department. Walking slowly and looking all around her, she headed down an aisle of lawn mowers and edge trimmers.

"Hello?" Sara called. "Please come out. I'm here if you want to talk to me."

As she spoke, she pulled out her phone. If any of them did decide to communicate, she wanted to be ready with the camera. It seemed the only way to hear their voices was to record them and play it back.

Sara wasn't sure why that was.

She stopped in the middle of the aisle and listened. The only sound she heard was the distant music coming from the break room where everyone was eating their pizza. The rest of the store was silent.

Sara even tried to see if she could detect a chill in the air, one of the biggest indicators that the ghost children were near.

"I know about the storm," Sara said, "and I'm sorry."

Somewhere to her left, she heard something slam. Sara was unsure if it was paranormal activity or if one of the inventory workers dropped something. Without stopping to overthink it, she rounded the end of the aisle to where she thought the noise came from and headed into the grocery section. She stopped at the end of the frozen foods aisle. Along both sides of the lane were freezers with glass doors, designed to let customers see the frosty products inside.

Sara opened and closed a door holding breakfast bowls and waffles. The noise sounded exactly like what she'd heard.

The aisle, however, was empty.

She walked down the middle of the aisle, glancing left and right at the frozen dinners, bags of vegetables, and chopped fruit. In the case holding the chicken pot-pies, she noticed a small handprint on the inside of the door.

It was as if someone very young had opened the door and pressed their hand against the condensation that formed there.

"Are you here right now?" Sara asked.

It was cooler in the aisle, but she didn't know if it meant a ghost was present or if it was just from the standing freezers.

Out of the corner of her left eye, she saw movement.

She watched as the word *yes* was written letter by letter inside another freezer door.

And as chilly as Sara was, she felt another level of cold wash over her.

Realizing she was still holding her phone, Sara switched it to camera mode and began recording. She grabbed some footage of the word *yes* before it faded

away. Her hand shook, and goose bumps dotted her forearms.

"My name is Sara," she said, hearing her voice waver. "What's your name?"

There was complete silence and Sara worried that she'd already scared the ghost child away.

She stared at the freezer door where she'd seen the handprint, then back to the one where *yes* had been written.

Are there two of them here?

Just as Sara was thinking they were gone, the name *Emma* appeared on one door. The name *Alice* appeared on another door across the aisle, but in a handwriting from someone who was just learning to print. She captured both on video.

"Emma and Alice," Sara whispered. "It's—it's nice to meet you."

You're losing it, Sara, she told herself.

As she stood there, the names began to fade into the condensation of the freezer doors. Sara looked to see if she could see the ghostly girls inside the coolers but couldn't spot any discernible humanlike features.

"How long have you been here?" Sara asked. She walked closer to the door where the name Emma had appeared.

There was another long pause and Sara felt the aisle grow even cooler. She didn't know if it was because of the freezers or if it was the touch of fear that made her skin tighten. Her throat felt dry and a shiver coursed through her, causing her phone to shake in her hand.

"Hello?" Sara called. She didn't want to seem impatient but wasn't sure if they'd left her in the frozen food aisle by herself.

The word s*torm* appeared in the condensation, one letter at a time.

"The Great Storm of 1900," Sara said. "I'm so sorry that happened to you."

Sara thought again of how scary it must have been for those children that day.

"If you're stuck here, I want to help you," Sara said. "Will you let me?"

Yes, came the first reply from Alice, written in her slightly messier scrawl.

"Good," Sara whispered. "Please let me do something. What is it you need?"

As Alice's reply faded away, Emma's began to form on her freezer door.

Not here.

"I don't understand," Sara said. "What's not here? You need something that's not in the store?"

It didn't make sense and her brain tried to think of anything and everything it could to figure out what they were trying to tell her.

Not here . . . Are they trying to say they don't want to be here?

That seemed to make the most sense. Suddenly she felt like she was getting somewhere.

"How can I help you get out of here?" Sara asked. Her voice was excited and almost desperate. "Help you leave the store?"

She glanced at both doors and finally saw Alice start to write her response.

S – T – O – R –

"Hey, Sara," a loud male voice called from behind her. "There you are. Your mom's looking for you."

Sara turned and saw Bobby coming her way.

No! She thought, then quickly glanced back at the freezer door. Alice never finished writing her message. She knew instantly that both of the ghost girls were gone, scared away by Bobby.

"Ugh," Sara groaned. She captured the fading word with her camera and then stopped recording.

"What are you doing down here?" Bobby asked, although he didn't seem interested in an answer. He pointed at the frozen pizzas. "There's still some pizza left in the break room if you're hungry."

"Oh, no thanks," Sara said. "I kind of lost my appetite." *And any real shot at figuring out what the ghosts were trying to tell me.*

She thanked Bobby for coming to find her and made her way back toward the front of the store.

Store? Storm? Were they just repeating what I said?

Sara found her mom in the break room, cleaning up the empty pizza boxes as the rest of the crew dispersed back into the store to finish taking inventory. She stuffed two boxes sideways into the garbage can next to the soda machine.

"Hey Mom," Sara said.

"Where have you been?" Mom asked. "I was going to have you help me with something."

Sara looked back over her shoulder toward the food section.

"I was talking with the ghosts," Sara said.

Her mom made a noise and muttered something under her breath in Chinese. Sara knew she only did that when she was losing her patience.

"I don't want to hear about these ghosts anymore," Mom said.

"But I actually caught some footage on my phone," Sara replied. She walked over to her mom and held her phone out. "It was a little boy who talked to me!"

Her mom wasn't interested. She turned her head and put her hand out as if to push Sara's screen away from her face.

"I don't want to see it, Sara," Mom said.

"But—" Sara cried.

"I leave them alone and they leave me alone," Mom replied. "It is bad luck to get involved with the dead."

Sara felt like she'd been punched in the stomach.

"You always knew about the ghosts?" Sara whispered. "You knew about them all along?"

Mom was quiet and went back to picking up the paper plates from off the table. She shoved them into the over-stuffed garbage bin.

"You used to celebrate the ghosts when you were a little girl in Hong Kong!" Sara cried. "The Hungry Ghost Buffet thing!"

"Hungry Ghost *Festival*," Mom corrected her. "And those were my relatives and your ancestors."

Sara was stunned. She didn't know what to say. And worst of all? She felt deeply disappointed in her mom.

"These were kids who died in a hurricane, Mom,"

Sara said. "Back in 1900, there was an orphanage right here where the store is. A big hurricane came and wiped them all out. There were ninety kids and ten nuns and then they were gone, just like that."

Mom stopped and took a deep breath as if trying to keep her composure. "I didn't know," she said. "And I'm very sorry to hear that happened to them. But we can't help the dead. If anything, interacting with these departed spirits can only bring more trouble."

"I wanted to try," Sara said. She suddenly felt defeated and sad. "I'm sorry."

"You have a beautiful heart, Sara," Mom said. "The best one."

Her mom came over and gave her a hug. It made her feel a little better, even if she still felt like she wanted to cry.

"Thanks, Mom."

———————

Twenty minutes later, Sara was sitting in her mom's office behind the keyboard of the computer. To get a jump on reconciling the inventory changes from the store being open earlier in the day, she had to key in numbers to adjust the previous night's totals.

It was dull, but easy work. Her mom left her to it

and went back out into the store to keep tabs on the rest of the inventory crew. It sounded like within the hour, they'd be finished up.

To keep herself awake, Sara listened to music on an internet radio station.

Even though she'd all but given up trying to help the ghosts, she couldn't help but think about the exchange she'd had with the two ghost girls in the frozen foods section.

Not here, Sara thought. *Is it because they don't want to be here at the store anymore? But what if that isn't it?*

She typed in another string of numbers from the log sheets her mom left for her. As she waited for them to process, Sara looked up and peered out through the two-way mirror. The store looked dim and empty. And, knowing what had happened over the last few nights, haunted.

Suddenly, her music cut out. The external speakers her mom had connected to the computer made a light static hissing noise. Sara glanced at them and the internet page from where she'd been streaming music. A giant circle spun in the middle of the screen.

SORRY! SOMETHING WENT WRONG! The error

screen said. It showed an old-time radio with smoke coming out of it.

Help us, a voice whispered through the speakers.

Sara rolled back in her chair, startled. She glanced up, and through the two-way mirror, she saw a small girl peering through the glass back at her.

When Sara stood up, the girl turned and walked through one of the cashier lanes and then turned back to see if Sara was following her.

It's time, a voice over the speaker said.

"Okay," Sara said.

As she walked to the door, the internet fired up and the music resumed playing.

Sara didn't look back as she left her mom's office.

CHAPTER 10

GOODNIGHT, CHILDREN

Sara walked through one of the self-checkout lanes to follow the small ghost girl. As she passed the touch-screen terminals, a waft of cool air washed over her. She studied the little spirit and noticed she was wearing a raincoat like some of the others had on earlier in the morning.

The little girl turned and waved Sara forward, urging her to keep following.

"Where are we going?" Sara asked. She wasn't surprised to see the little girl's mouth open, but no sound came out. Sara patted her back pocket and realized she'd left her phone on her mom's desk.

I can't go back now, Sara thought. *Something tells me I'm not going to need it.*

As she reached the main aisle that ran behind the checkout lanes, Sara heard her mom talking to George and froze in place. She knew that her mom would not be

117

happy with her if she knew she'd abandoned her work and was off following ghosts around the store again.

Moving quickly, she dashed across the aisle and slid behind a large display of discount DVDs and Blu-ray discs. She pressed her back up against the bin and listened to hear if her mom was coming toward her. As she did, she saw the little girl standing near the cereal and breakfast aisle in the grocery section. She stood and watched Sara quietly.

She can't be more than five years old, Sara realized. It still pained her to think of how terrified the orphans must have been that horrible night. *Young or old, the hurricane didn't care.*

Footsteps approached, and she held her breath, keeping as still as possible. She didn't know if it was her mom or George coming her way, but only hoped they would pass by without noticing. Sara kept her eye on the little girl too. She was certain whoever was coming would scare her off.

A moment later, George walked by, headed for the men's clothing department. He was messing with something on his inventory scanner and never even noticed Sara, who was crouching behind the DVDs.

Once he had passed, Sara stood up and turned back

toward the last spot she'd seen the ghost. To her amazement, the little girl was still waiting for her.

The faded spirit waved her on. *C'mon,* she seemed to say.

Sara peered around the corner to make sure her mom wasn't looking her way. When she saw the coast was clear, she dashed across the wide main aisle and into the breakfast section.

The little girl walked along, never looking back. She reached the end of the aisle and continued through the home goods area. Sara paused again to look around to make sure she wasn't spotted. She saw Shonda scanning shelves of bathroom towels across the way.

As the little girl passed a towel display, Shonda shivered and rubbed her arms as if to warm up. Completely unaware that a spirit was only a few feet away from her, she continued scanning the shelves of colorful towels.

Sara followed the little girl until they were on the edge of the home department and across from another main aisle that steered customers to electronics, toys, and the Halloween costumes and decor.

Where is she taking me?

Sara passed the aisle where she'd started working the night before. It seemed like weeks had passed since she'd discovered the first little boy. She couldn't believe it had only been one day.

The little girl walked down the main aisle as if she wasn't concerned about being seen. She continued past toys to a small section just before electronics. There were shelves displaying the newest CDs, movies, and television shows. One shelf over, was an endcap that held newly released books.

The girl stopped and gazed down the aisle.

What is she looking at?

As Sara got closer to the ghost girl, she felt a bone-deep chill. The girl walked slowly down the aisle and looked at the shelves of books on either side. She stopped and turned to watch Sara follow her.

"I don't understand," Sara said. "What am I supposed—"

Before she could finish asking her question, a book fell onto the floor from the shelf on her left. Then another. A large picture book dropped on the right from a lower shelf. A couple more fell from shelves further down the aisle.

They were all kids' books.

"Why are you doing this?" Sara asked.

Sara began to walk down the aisle. She stopped at the first book that lay on the floor. It landed facedown. She picked it up and turned it over. On the cover was an illustration of a large adult zebra reading to a young zebra lying in bed.

"*20 Best Bedtime Stories,*" she read aloud.

She thought back to what the little boy said in the video she made. Sara remembered asking him what he needed.

"We want sleep. But we can't without our bedtime . . ."

Suddenly, it dawned on Sara what Alice, who wrote *S-T-O-R* on the condensation on the freezer door, was trying to tell her.

"You want me to read you a bedtime story," she finally said.

The girl's blurry eyes widened, and her head nodded up and down. She pointed at the thick volume in Sara's hands. The chill in the air grew as a ghost boy arrived at the other end of the aisle. A cluster of ghost girls approached from the other end. Other children materialized through the shelves to join the rest.

"Oh," Sara gasped. "Oh wow."

She watched as spirits only a few years younger than her joined the little ghost children. Some were wearing their raincoats. Others were dressed in the same white shirt and dark pants she had seen before.

Soon there were ghosts everywhere, more than Sara had ever seen. They were packed in together. Some sat on the floor, others were sitting on the shelves. It felt like a small arena and Sara was center stage.

Sara's heart raced as the cold emanating from the ghosts enveloped her. She turned and saw that all of them were looking at her. Waiting.

Sara pulled up a chair from the display at the end of the aisle and cracked open the book. If it was going to be story time, she wanted it to be authentic, like the story times her dad used to bring her to at the Rosenberg Library when she was little.

Sara shivered in the cold as she flipped to the table of contents. She didn't know which story to read, so she went with one she thought sounded funny.

"This one is called 'Stay Awake Jake,'" Sara said.

The spirits leaned forward to listen. Some of them looked at each other as if excited for Sara to begin.

"There was a little boy, who lived by a lake," Sara read aloud, "who had blond hair, and his parents called Jake."

She held up the book and showed them a picture of the little boy in the book. He looked sleepy but determined to keep from falling asleep.

"It was Jake's birthday and for his own sake, he tried his best to stay awake."

Sara continued, reading how Jake ate his entire birthday cake, sat on a rake, wrestled with a snake, and jumped in the lake in an effort to make sure he didn't sleep through his party.

She showed them every picture and read slowly and

carefully to make sure each of the ghost children could hear the story. All of them sat riveted in the afterlife until Sara reached the end where, despite all his efforts, little Jake finally fell asleep.

"The end," Sara said. She showed them all the final picture of Jake asleep on top of his bed with a birthday hat on.

As she spoke the last words and closed the book, something happened. Through the display of mystery novels along the back wall emerged several taller, darker figures. They were hooded in black. Sara's heart began to race.

Once they were completely in view, Sara saw who they were.

"The nuns," she whispered, standing up.

Ten nuns stood along the back wall, almost if they were forming a passageway there. They stood with their hands clasped in front of them, waiting. One by one, the children stood up and walked single file between the nuns. Sara watched as the first twenty children disappeared through the wall.

With each child who departed, she could feel the air and mood of the book aisle change. It became warmer by the second, and the heaviness that hung around the store seemed to lessen with every moment.

Some of them looked back at Sara and smiled, as if grateful for what she'd done.

Sara returned the smile, holding the book in her hands as they passed through to the other side.

The little girl who led Sara to story time was the last in line. As the girl approached the wall, she turned and looked at Sara for a moment. The girl raised her hand in a wave and mouthed something Sara didn't need her phone to hear.

"You're welcome," Sara said, smiling and waving back. "And good night, Alice."

The girl smiled, then walked through the wall and disappeared. The nuns all nodded to Sara before turning to follow the children. Sara watched as they faded away.

Sara stood staring at the mystery book display for a moment and took a deep breath. The store was somehow different now. There were no ghosts left.

They were free.

As Sara bent to pick up all the books that had fallen from the shelves, she saw her mom standing at the end of the aisle. Her eyes were wide and maybe even a little teary. Sara wasn't sure how long she had been there, but clearly it had been long enough.

"I'm sorry Mom," Sara began. "But I had to."

Her mom shook her head as if what Sara had to say wasn't important. She walked to Sara and gave her a hug.

"They just wanted a bedtime story," Sara said into her mom's shoulder. "They couldn't rest until they had it."

Her mom hugged her tighter.

"I'm sorry I doubted what you could do," Mom said, finally releasing Sara from her grasp. "But when I asked you to help us out tonight, I had no idea you'd be able to help those poor little souls too. I believe you've helped them all find peace, Sara."

Sara smiled and looked toward the wall.

"I hope so," Sara said. "I guess some spirits are hungry and some just need to hear a bedtime story before they rest."

AUTHOR'S NOTE

More often than not, stories about hauntings always seem to happen in old, creepy-looking places that just *look* like they should be haunted. When I discovered the story about the Great Storm of 1900 and St. Mary's Orphanage, I knew I'd found something different.

The Great Storm of 1900 was one of the worst in recorded history in terms of loss of life. It's believed that between six thousand and eight thousand people died in the storm. Though they didn't have technology to predict the storm, the US Weather Bureau warned people to move to higher ground. The warnings were mostly ignored. The hurricane was a Category 4 storm, which is classified as "major" and can generate winds up from 130 to 156 miles per hour. The Great Storm produced a fifteen-foot surge that flooded the city. Ships from the Gulf were tossed around like toys. One of the ships struck the boys' dormitory of the orphanage, causing the floor to drop out beneath the children. The roof collapsed, trapping the boys in the water.

I honestly have no idea if the ghosts in this story were waiting for their bedtime story, but I did learn that to keep the kids calm while the storm raged on outside, the nuns had them sing a song together. They sang a French hymn called "Queen of the Waves." And each nun really did tie a clothesline around the waists of six to eight orphans so they could all stay together.

As you can probably guess, ValueMart isn't a real place, but there is a very similar store that sits on the exact site. Employees and customers have noticed strange things happening in the store, including misplaced toys, laughter, and cries for help.

Galveston is known as one of the most haunted cities in the United States, and the spot where this store is located is considered the most haunted location on the island. In 1994, on the anniversary of the Great Storm, the state of Texas placed a historical marker on the original site of the St. Mary's Orphan Asylum. It details the storm and the heroic efforts of the nuns who tried to save the children

Even though Sara helped the St. Mary's Orphanage ghosts in this book, a few questions remain here in the real world. Why are there still ghosts at the store in Galveston, Texas? Are they waiting for something? If you ever stop at the store to pick up a few things, maybe you can ask them and find out!

ABOUT THE AUTHOR

Thomas Kingsley Troupe has been making up stories ever since he was in short pants. As an "adult," he's the author of a whole lot of books for kids. When he's not writing, he enjoys movies, biking, taking naps, and investigating ghosts as a member of the Twin Cities Paranormal Society. Raised in "Nordeast" Minneapolis, he now lives in Woodbury, Minnesota, with his awe-inspiring family.

ABOUT THE ILLUSTRATOR

Maggie Ivy is a freelance illustrator and artist who lives and works in the Ozark area in Arkansas. She found her love for art at an early age and pursued it with passion. She graduated from The Florence Academy of Art in 2010. She loves narrative elements and story-building moments, and seeks to implement them in her own work.

Take a sneak peek at an excerpt from
Trapped in Room 217, another spine-tingling tale in
the Haunted States of America series.

———————

Despite having a pretty heavy comforter on the bed, Jayla was cold. She opened her eyes, fairly certain that her little brother had rolled himself up in the thick blanket. A second later, she realized that wasn't the case. She had plenty of covers on her side of the bed.

The *room* was cold.

Jayla sat up slightly and nearly shrieked at what she saw.

There was a woman in their room.

Before Jayla could move or make a sound, the woman walked toward her side of the bed until she was standing almost next to her. Waves of cold and terror washed over Jayla as she slipped her face under the covers. She considered covering herself completely to hide, but couldn't. Something inside her told her that she needed to watch this woman.

She's a ghost, Jayla thought. *There's a ghost in our room!*

Everything in her wanted to throw the light on and scream to wake her dad and brother up, but she couldn't. Though she'd never been paralyzed and didn't know exactly what that was like, that's how she felt. She was stuck.

As her pounding heart threatened to burst, Jayla noticed something different about the lady. Jayla could see right through her to the door on the other side of the room. Even so, she could make out the clothes the lady was wearing. It looked like an old-time maid's uniform. She wore a dark long-sleeved dress with white straps that connected to an apron around her waist. On top of her head was a white bonnet-like hat.

The maid didn't look at Jayla, which made it a little easier for her to watch the mysterious visitor, but not much. Even though the figure didn't seem to want to harm her, Jayla was afraid to look away. The woman's dark eyes looked ahead to the wall next to the bed, and Jayla could make out some of the details in her face. She was a younger lady, probably in her mid-twenties. Her eyes seemed empty and her mouth held tight as if she was concentrating on something.

Please don't hurt us, Jayla thought, shivering under her heavy blankets.

She watched as the maid reached her hand up to the wall, holding it there a moment. The maid then turned and walked back toward the door to the hallway, but paused halfway in between. She crouched down and Jayla held her breath.

She's going under the bed, she thought. *The ghost is going to hide under the bed and get us when I'm asleep again.*

Before Jayla could even think to scream, the maid stood up again. She brushed her skirt straight with her hands and walked out, passing through the closed door.

The room was silent and still. Jayla exhaled, realizing how long she'd held her breath. After a moment, the chill in the air dissipated and it seemed like the world, at least the world inside of Room 217, went back to normal.

Dion grunted a little and flipped over to his side. Her dad's soft snores drifted through the darkness. Jayla was pretty sure she could hear her heart rapidly drum the inside of her ribcage.

She lay there motionless, afraid to move or do anything short of breathing. What would happen if she got up? If she woke up her dad to let him know what she'd seen, would the ghostly maid come back? Could she hurt them somehow?

I hate this place, Jayla decided. She'd had an uneasy feeling about the hotel before, but just then, she realized why. It was haunted and they were stuck there for the whole week.

At night, Dion sometimes liked to climb into bed with her when he was scared. Suddenly, she knew how he felt. Jayla was tempted to wake him up so that she didn't feel so frightened and alone.

I can't do that, Jayla realized. *He's going to be even more scared if I tell him what I've seen. He'll never be able to get to sleep and he'll be a nightmare to watch tomorrow when Dad's at work. I need to pull it together and be brave. That's all there is to it.*

Jayla looked over to where the ghost had passed through the closed door and into the hallway. There didn't seem to be any sign of the paranormal visitor, and the room didn't feel as chilly as it had before. She just hoped that meant the ghost was gone for good.

Wanting to prove to herself that she wasn't scared, Jayla pulled the covers aside for a moment. Taking a deep breath, she swung her legs out from under the covers and placed her bare feet on the floor. The carpet felt soft and warm, as if the room had not been icy cold only moments before.

Maybe I just dreamed the whole thing, Jayla thought. *Or maybe at age twelve, I'm already starting to go a little crazy!*

She stood up and walked toward the bathroom door. It was still closed and she was thankful for that. If it was open and dark inside, just about anything could jump out at her without warning. If something opened the door, at least she'd have a second to turn and run.

But the ghost didn't open the door, Jayla reminded herself.

She shook her head slightly, trying to knock the dumb thoughts from her head. Jayla reminded herself to be brave, not talk herself into being terrified by something she might or might not have seen.

With new determination, Jayla walked slowly along the side of the bed. When she reached the end, she put her hand on the thick wooden bedpost. She stopped to listen for any weird noises, but the room was mostly silent.

Jayla decided what she would do. She'd look out into the hallway to see if the ghost was out there. Though she wasn't sure what she'd do if she *did* see the spooky maid, at least she'd be able to know whether she was just seeing things.

As she took another step past the little bench at the end of the bed, the floor beneath her feet creaked. It took everything in her to not shriek, dive back under the covers, and never come out again.

Instead, she exhaled nice and slow and closed her eyes for a moment. The room didn't get cold again, and she didn't feel that strange tingle down her back. Other than her brother and dad, she was alone and nothing was happening.

Jayla opened her eyes and let them readjust to the little bit of light coming through the window. She continued to the door and paused. She hadn't noticed before, but their room didn't have a peephole to look out into the hallway. They usually made everything look distorted, as if peering through a fish-eye lens.

If she wanted to look outside, she'd have to open the door.

I have to know, Jayla decided. *Even if it might wake up Dion and Dad.*

She reached down and undid the lock, trying as carefully as she could to be quiet. It released with a soft *thunk* and she turned the knob. Jayla could only pray that there wouldn't be a spooky face waiting for her on the other side.

Slowly, she opened the door, letting a tiny sliver of light into their room. She squinted from the lights in the hallway.

Want to read what happens next?
Check out *Trapped in Room 217* and the rest of the Haunted States of America series.

J Troupe Thomas
Troupe, Thomas Kingsley,
Spirits of the storm /
22960001680718
                    ACL-IVA